let it
SHINE

ALYSSA

*The most common way people give up
their power is by thinking they don't have any.*
-Alice Walker

chapter one

Sofie usually felt at peace after church—there was comfort in the rote liturgical acts, and in the familiarity of her fellow parishioners. She sorely needed that familiarity after almost two semesters of college at Virginia Union, where she felt more out of place than she ever had. But for some reason, Ms. Simcox's pained repetition of "Praise Jesus" hadn't made her giggle, as it had when she was a girl; instead, she nodded along at the soul-weary sound. Reverend Mills' showmanship and bluster, which often made her suppress an eye roll, resonated with something deep inside of her this time.

"Change is coming!" he'd shouted while mopping his brow. "If you believe in the power of God Almighty, you know that change is on the way!" A chill had gone through her as those words rang through the small church, echoed by the approving shouts and soft murmurs of the congregation. Sofie didn't know if Reverend Mills could actually channel the will of the Lord, but his words seemed like an answer to the doubt that had been gnawing at her all semester.

You went to school to learn, not to fight. Her father's words echoed in her head. *You know better than anyone what fighting gets you.*

Sofie glanced at her father across the basement of the church, where he sat with his brows drawn, shaking his head at something one of his friends was saying. She wished, just once, that she would look over and see him laughing like he used to.

"They finally let that child out of jail today," Mrs. Pierce said, pulling Sofie back to the after-church social gathering. "It wasn't right for them white folk to arrest her, but Patty knows better. The girl can read! Had the nerve to sit right under the 'Whites Only' sign, like she was daring them." The woman ran an age-spotted but manicured hand over her exquisitely coiffed gray hair, and passed a plate of food to one of the visiting pastors working his way down the buffet line. The young man accepted it with a gracious nod and a lingering glance at Sofie, who was just the right age to attract the attentions of promising young men in need of a good, obedient wife. Sofie scooped a spoonful of macaroni and cheese and let it fall to his Styrofoam plate with a moist plop. He fumbled to keep the plate from tipping and moved on.

"She lost the baby, you know, after they threw her off that bus," Melba Adams said in a hushed tone. Sofie almost dropped the next spoonful of food she was distributing. Her usually steady hand was shaking like old Mr. Duffy's when he needed a nip but couldn't afford it. Melba shook her head sadly. "It's sad, but I can't help but think it's for the best. The Lord works in mysterious ways, and she was awful young to be having a baby."

The women continued gossiping, but Sofie felt the bite of food she'd snuck earlier rising up her throat. Patty's baby was dead? She couldn't call the younger girl a friend, exactly, but just last week—in this very room—Sofie had felt that baby move. She'd felt its enthusiastic kick right against her palm. Why was everyone acting like that was okay?

Sofie felt a pressure building up in her chest, a burning hot anger that surprised her. She didn't get mad. Everyone knew that, and if everyone knew it, it must be true. Just like everyone knew that a black girl who sat at the front of the bus deserved whatever she got for causing trouble. The belt that cinched Sofie's favorite blue dress suddenly seemed too tight.

She took a small, tight breath and tried to calm herself, an act that was second nature to her by now. It was why, when people described her, they used words like *nice* and *quiet* and *docile* as if they spoke of the cows on Harris Withers' farm instead of a young woman. She should've been happy—that was what she'd wanted, right? For everyone to see how good she was? But, if Sofie were honest with herself, she'd felt like none of those things lately. Every time she had to give up her seat on the bus, she considered saying no. Every time a store clerk followed her as if she had the word CRIMINAL stamped on her forehead, she wanted to whirl and demand they leave her be. And every time a group of men, white men usually, shouted crude insults from their car and made her fear the worst, then she wished she could damn them to hell herself without waiting for God's plodding judgment.

Mrs. Pierce snorted in a most unladylike way. "Awful young? How about awful fast?"

"Oh, come on now, Sister Pierce," Leonia Grant said, with a hand on her hip. "Tread lightly."

"You know these fast-tailed girls are always getting themselves into trouble," Mrs. Pierce said with an elegant shrug as if that explained everything.

Usually, Sofie would have just listened to the women gossip and ignored the urge to give her own opinion, but the new anger in her was a grease fire that wouldn't be doused. It bubbled and popped, pushing angry words out of her mouth like they were too hot to be contained in the caldron of her chest. "If she's fast, what would you call the man twice her age who put the baby in her? A speed demon?"

She almost laughed when all of the women's heads whipped in her direction. "Sofronia Wallis! Hush, now," Melba said, her eyes wide. Sofie glanced across the room, where the man in question was showering his attentions on yet another girl young enough to be his daughter. They were only worried he would hear, she realized, not that he'd offered Patty help with her singing and gotten her with child instead. Melba looked at Sofie again. "What's gotten into you?"

"Not Jim Danielson, and thank goodness for that. Otherwise, I'd be the one you all were showing such kind Christian compassion for." Somewhere inside of her, the old Sofie was already cowering and begging forgiveness. That Sofie was worrying about what her father would say when, not if, word of her rudeness got to him. But the grease fire in her chest was still going, fueled by thoughts of Patty and the little baby who would never get to grow up. By the pictures in the papers of white folk beating people who looked just like her as the police looked on with smiles. Sofie felt like she would combust from the unfairness of it all.

Mrs. Pierce pulled her shoulders back. "How is it that you can't get out more than a squeak at choir practice, yet here you are now trying to get involved in grown folks' business?"

It seemed Mrs. Pierce, who also served as choir director, would never forgive Sofie for the fact that the young woman's promising voice had gone silent right around the time when it should have been coming into its own, as if it had been a tributary of the river that was her mother's powerful contralto and had dried up when the woman passed on.

Heat streaked up Sofie's neck and warmed her face, and she shoved the spoon into the pan of macaroni. "I don't feel well. Please excuse me." With that, she turned and walked across the basement of the church, sure that a tsunami of gossip was building behind her and would soon arrive at her shores, courtesy of a scolding from her father. She trotted up the stairs, her long pleated skirt swishing around her calves.

When she stepped outside into the warm spring afternoon, she felt she could finally breathe again. The fringe tree flowers scenting the breeze seemed to clear the troublesome thoughts from her mind.

She closed her eyes for a moment, feeling utterly alone. She hadn't ever felt like this when Mama was alive. Even though Delia Wallis had died years and years ago, and everyone told her that God didn't make mistakes, Sofie still resented her absence. *Mama would know what to do. She always knew. If only—*

Sofie cringed at the thought that assailed her then, shoved it away into that hot place inside her; maybe her anger could burn it up and make it so she never thought about that horrible day again. But even if she forgot, her father never would.

After her mother's death, Mr. Wallis had embarked on a mission: to raise a respectable black woman. Not just a good, God-fearing woman, but the kind her mama used to roll her eyes at in the supermarket and department stores. Thus, each Christmas from the age of twelve on, Sofie received prim new dress patterns and a new etiquette book. Sofie loved making her own clothing, but the books were worse than anything her teachers could dole out. The first had been *The Practical Self-Educator*. On her eighteenth birthday, she'd unwrapped *Golden Thoughts on Chastity and Procreation* and nearly died of embarrassment. That had been the last one, two years ago, as if everything she needed to know stopped with tips on how to keep herself chaste for marriage.

It was like Daddy had forgotten how Mama always pushed Sofie to speak out, to take guff from no one. The last time Sofie had tried to make her mama proud had been the day her mother died. Sofie had felt the anger grow in her chest, the same that she felt now, and she'd done something a little black girl was never supposed to do: stand up for herself. The screaming, red-faced boys who'd been attacking Ivan, her mother's charge, had turned on her, too. When her mother ran out to stop the melee, she'd collapsed in the middle of them; her mama's last moment had been loud, frightening, and humiliating.

The doctors said it was an aneurysm, but Sofie had thought of something her Sunday school teacher often said: "God don't like ugly." So she accepted her etiquette books gladly, and read them until the pages were worn thin. She sewed her dresses with skirts well below the knee and made sure to wear her gloves and hat. Her hair was always pressed straight, or pin-curled just so. She nodded along when the women at her church told her the rules she would have to follow forever. But now the anger was back for some reason, and she knew that the solution to her particular problem wasn't covered in any of her rule books.

"Lord, please tell me what to do," she whispered, crossing her arms over the starched fabric of her dress. The buttons pressed into her arms as she waited, but as in every other instance, she got no reply. She opened her eyes and shook her head, and was about to laugh at herself when a sign pinned to the center of the community message board caught her eye.

MEETING:
TONIGHT, MAY 12, AT 7:30
COMMUNITY CENTER, ROOM 203
STUDENT NONVIOLENT COORDINATING
COMMITTEE
TAKE A STAND AGAINST INJUSTICE

Sofie knew what those kinds of meetings entailed. Her friend Henrietta was involved, and her friend David, Henrietta's boyfriend, was a coordinator. Sofie always wanted to say "yes" when Henrietta invited her to come out, but things were different for her. Henrietta's parents were involved in the movement. Sofie's father railed about protestors causing trouble for good black folk who kept their heads down and worked hard. She would gently remind him that there was plenty of trouble before folk started protesting, but he was stubborn as a mule.

Sofie glanced at the sign again. Protesting was something that wasn't covered in any of her etiquette books, and if it were it would definitely fall under the "detrimental to the race" category, but just thinking of going to the meeting filled her with a sense of excitement and purpose that she hadn't felt since...ever.

What Daddy doesn't know won't hurt him, she thought as she returned to the church gathering to make amends for her outburst. That was what a good girl would do, after all.

chapter two

S of!" Henrietta whispered fiercely, throwing out an elbow that caught Sofie in the ribs. "What are you looking at, girl? If you want to volunteer, you have to *listen*." She looked suspiciously at the crowd, as if trying to spot who'd caught her friend's eye.

Sofie winced, rubbing at her side. Her friend was soft and curvy in all the right places, with the exclusion of her razor-sharp elbows.

"I'm listening," she whispered back. And she had been. The little notebook she always carried with her for making lists was open in her lap, and notes covered the page. But she'd also been unable to tear her eyes away from the man across the room, the tall one with dark hair and dolorous eyes who leaned against the wall, listening intently to whoever had the floor at a given moment. There was a quiet intensity to his attention, as if he was turning over what each speaker said and carefully fitting it into some bigger picture.

She didn't know why her gaze sought him out—she told herself it was only because he was one of the few white men in the room, and thus he stood out as an anomaly. But she knew that wasn't true. A simple anomaly wouldn't make her breath catch and her palms sweat in her gloves. There was something about him, but she couldn't pinpoint it.

Most of the young people in the room were dressed in suits that screamed respectability, but he wore dark denim pants and a simple white t-shirt. Sofie had a feeling that was his idea of dressing up. He brought a hand up to rub at his eye, and Sofie saw they were large, with bruises fading away at the knuckles. There was a bump on the bridge of his nose that hinted it'd been broken, and probably more than once. Paired with the dark half-moon under his right eye, she could draw one conclusion: he was a fighter. Even that intense gaze of his showed that he brooked no resistance. What was a man like him doing at a meeting for nonviolent protestors?

His head turned slowly, but with such precise motion that it seemed sudden, and his gaze connected with hers. Heat rose to Sofie's cheeks, but she held their stare-down for a moment longer. The etiquette books said staring was impolite, but she'd been impolite all day and was rather liking it. The stranger's lips pulled up at the corners, but not in a friendly way. His smile made her think of sucking honey straight from the comb, of the sweetness spreading on your tongue and how it could make you smile like that; like you'd just tasted something real good and wanted more.

A low, sultry sound rose up in her throat, the kind a woman made to let you know she was about to belt out a tune that would make you blush. It was an uncharacteristic sound for Sofie, who was the bane of every choirmaster due to her stubborn refusal to project her voice. Luckily, it blended with the sounds of the students who were giving David their full attention, supporting him with cries of "Yes, brother!" and "Preach!"

Sofie turned back to pay attention to David, who was working the crowd with that gentle but powerful voice of his. David, with his reddish-brown skin, nearly the color of the brick building where they'd shared their first—and last—kiss. They'd been children then, though, only fourteen. She'd gotten over her childhood crush, and David had recently found happiness with Henrietta. She was elated for her friends, if not a little bit envious. She ignored the loneliness that enveloped her like the darkness of her bedroom when she woke in the night, the kind she wasn't sure came from a lack of light or from something dark and undeserving of God's grace inside her.

"Now, ya'll believe you know what you're getting into, but I ask that you think long and hard." David's father was a preacher, and he'd inherited the man's booming voice and magnetic personality. "Have you seen the pictures in the paper of what's happening at the sit-ins across the South? Someone might call you a nigger, or pour ketchup on you, and maybe you can handle that." He looked around encouragingly before quickly drawing his brows into an accusatory expression. "But if you want to participate, you need to be sure that you can deal with a white man calling your mother a whore as he punches you in the head. With a mob pulling you to the ground and stomping you into unconsciousness. With someone punching your girl or grabbing her breast and calling her a jezebel. Can you deal with that and not fight back?" He cast a long look over the crowd. Some of the men grumbled and shook their heads. Sofie risked a glance at the fighter and caught his gaze sliding away from her; he was watching her, too. She plucked at the pleats in her skirt and shifted in her seat.

Her thoughts were a muddle. When she'd decided to go to the meeting, she hadn't understood exactly what she was getting into; this was a dangerous thing the students were planning to do. To sit where they weren't allowed or wanted, to be still no matter what was unleashed upon them. Henrietta had mentioned that the group needed help with administrative tasks and fundraising, and even though just attending had been an act of defiance, Sofie thought maybe she could help with that. Daddy couldn't get mad about shuffling papers, could he? But as she listened to speaker after speaker recount the latest acts of resistance, the confusion that'd been twisting her inside out transformed into excitement. Could she ever be brave enough to do such a thing? Maybe she could.

"That's all for tonight," David said from the front of the room. "For those interested in the sit-in and other activities, please come to the training session two days from now. You can get the details from Henny. I can't say it'll be fun, but you'll learn right quick whether you're cut out for this or not." He rubbed his jaw, perhaps thinking of a training session that had ended in a scuffle. Sofie glanced at her fighter—*not mine*, she corrected—but he simply looked amused.

Henrietta was pulled into the crowd, her formidable organizational skills obvious in the way she deftly handled the dozens of questions being hurled at her without mussing her curls. Sofie thought she might faint to have that much attention on her all at once, to be the one people turned to for guidance. But still…David's words tumbled around in her mind, ricocheting around like the pinball game she sometimes played at the Student Union.

She sat in her seat and looked at her gloved hands as she waited for the meeting to die down. When a set of bruised knuckles came into her peripheral vision, she willed herself not to look up. For one thrilling moment, she thought he would stop beside her. Hoped he would stop, really. Maybe she *was* going crazy. He kept walking, saving her the trouble of finding out how she would've reacted.

"You okay, Sof?" When she looked up David was there, concern evident in the crease of his brow. Most of the other people had milled out while she'd been deep in thought.

"That was a lot of information to absorb. I just need some air, I think," she said, standing to join them as they climbed the stairs.

"I was surprised to see you here, to be honest," he said. "But I'm glad you came. We can use all the administrative help we can get." It annoyed her that he assumed she wouldn't do any more than filing papers. But then she remembered the last eight years of her life—David was only acting on the information she'd provided to him. When they reached his car, the metallic monster that ferried people to and from the meeting, there was already a crowd surrounding it. Sofie couldn't stand the thought of being pressed against anyone while she felt so ready to jump out of her skin.

"You all go ahead. I'll just walk. I only live a few minutes from here, you know."

"Walk?" Henrietta asked. "Haven't you heard what happened to that woman on Ryan Road last week? A car full of white boys pulled over and snatched her, attacked her right in the woods over there. The cops don't care either, even though she knows the ones who did it."

Sofie reflexively clutched her hand to her heart. Not out of shock—this type of thing happened too often for her to be shocked—but out of pity. Still, she was feeling rebellious. Let someone try to snatch her. With all this anger pent up inside her, she'd kill them.

"There's no room for me," she said.

"You can ride with me, if you want."

It didn't take every set of eyes widening in disbelief for Sofie to know who the rough voice belonged to. She turned and found herself face to face with the man she'd been studying all evening long. She knew it was wrong, but she felt another type of warmth now, one that had nothing to do with anger and settled somewhere in the vicinity of an area proper women never discussed.

She felt an arm go around her. "Sofie doesn't take rides from strangers." Henrietta's tone was crisp enough that she didn't have to add the words *especially white ones* for everyone to get her point.

"Strangers?" The man never took his eyes off her. He grinned, revealing a chipped tooth, and a memory flashed through Sofie's mind. A skinny young boy flying over the handlebars of his bike, her mother running over and cradling him in her arms.

No. It couldn't be.

She allowed herself to feel a little bit of relief, right next to the anxiety and nostalgia this suddenly familiar man drew from her. Now she understood why her gaze had been drawn to him. Well, in part.

"You really don't remember me, Sofronia?" He laughed, a sound that was familiar and not at the same time, just like the rest of him. He was too tall now, and too muscular, and too handsome to be who she thought he was. He flashed that chipped tooth again, and she looked past the bruised face and stubbled cheeks and knew where she had seen those eyes that bored right into her. "I guess I have changed a bit," he said. "You look the same." The way he said "the same" should have been an insult considering that she'd been twelve when he last saw her, but there was a lift of the brow that showed appreciation.

"Black girls can't be princesses, Ivan." They'd been playing in the woods behind his parents' house, despite her mother's warning. He had looked over at her, teeth too big and eyes too wide. "Well, Jews can't be Nazi hunters, but I'm the best there is!" He'd run ahead a few steps, spraying down a line of imaginary SS men with his imaginary gun, then looked back at her. "Besides, every beautiful girl can be a princess. I read it in a book."

Sofie pulled herself back to the present. Murmurs passed through the students getting ready to leave, and some hung out of their car windows to get a better view. Oh God, they were creating a scene. A good young lady never allowed herself to be the center of attention, but Sofie couldn't help the way she gawped at the man.

She felt like a frayed rope threateningly close to unraveling as the realization hit her. She thought maybe she *should* just fall apart; then people could finally see all the hurt that hid away beneath her precisely sewn dresses, perfectly curled hair, and hats that tilted just so.

"You know this guy?" David asked, obviously wary.

Sofie nodded. Her head felt strangely heavy on her neck, like it might tumble off if she kept bobbing like a fool instead of speaking.

"Ivan?" Her voice shook, drawing the name out to four syllables instead of two.

He smiled again, but it was a soft one this time, tinged with pity. In that moment, she remembered that she hadn't been the only one to mourn Delia Wallis's loss.

Sofie thought she would faint. Instead she pasted on the smile that had gotten her through adolescence and into adulthood. "My mother worked for his family, the Friedmans, and we used to play together when we were younger," she explained to everyone in a tone that she hoped indicated finality.

He's the reason she's dead. But Sofie knew that wasn't fair. *It's because of him that I killed her.*

"Aren't you the guy who knocked out Knuckles Nelson two weeks ago?" One of the male volunteers pushed through the crowd and stared at Ivan with open admiration. "Man, the way you let him think he had you hemmed up, then walloped him!" The kid reenacted the moves as he talked.

Ivan ran a hand over the back of his neck with embarrassed pride. "Yeah, that was me."

Well, that explained his bruising.

"Oh, I've seen you fight before. Didn't recognize you outside the ring," David said. "This guy might could give Sugar Ray a run for his money if he had the chance."

"Trust me, I'm working on it," he said with a smile. Then he looked at Sofie. "You still need a ride?" He asked like it was something normal, but just the thought of being alone with him made her feel like her dress was two sizes too small. Having that intense gaze settle on her with an audience was making her feel burst open and exposed; if they were alone…

Ivan leaned forward a bit, raising one brow in a way she remembered so well now. "I have my dad's car, and it would be nice to catch up. Anyone else who needs a ride is welcome, too, of course."

"Actually, I'll just squeeze in with the others. Thanks anyway, though." She rushed around David's car, putting the hunk of metal between her and the man who was dredging up both unwanted memories and new sensations that were truly unfamiliar to her.

A couple of younger boys migrated over to Ivan, opening up more room in David's car. Ivan nodded, then gave her a little salute. "See you around."

That should have been a threat, but a not so small part of Sofie hoped he was right.

chapter three

Ivan never slept well, but the night after that first meeting was a fever dream of tossing and turning that'd seemed never-ending. He needed to be in top shape for his upcoming match; he should have been watching reels and making notes of Calvin Jones's techniques, but he'd accomplished none of that.

The few scraps of sleep he'd been able to snatch had thrown him for a loop: dreams of Sofronia, or Sofie as she was called now, had left him tossing and turning. She ran from him through one fantastic landscape after another, as if afraid he'd hurt her, but when he caught her she didn't seem to want to be anywhere else. He hadn't dreamed like that—soft curves and wide brown eyes as he plunged into warmth—since he was a teenager waking up in the night to sticky sheets. It had been her haunting his dreams then, too.

He didn't know why the urge to go to her after the meeting had been so strong or why, when all those skeptical faces had turned to him in the parking lot, he'd wanted it known that his acquaintance with her preceded all of theirs. He hadn't spoken to Sofie for eight years now, double the amount of time they'd spent together as children, but a stupid little thing like time hadn't changed the way he felt about her. His mother had called it a childhood crush, and clucked a laugh every time he mentioned Sofie's name with adulation. His father had told him to stay away from *those people* and chided his mom for not being more careful. Ivan had never stopped thinking of her.

Every time he taped his hands up before a fight, he thought of how weak he'd been the last day they'd played together. Every time he twisted and jabbed, and especially when he took a hit, he thought of how she'd stepped in front of the mob of neighborhood boys who'd grabbed up his arms and his legs, shouting, "We'll put you in the oven, where your kind belongs!" She'd used her fists to protect him, and then Miss Delia had come running from the house. He'd thought she'd make everything right, but the woman who had always been so strong froze and tumbled to the ground instead, sending the neighborhood boys scattering to the winds, their chests heaving with laughs of disbelief. "Did you see that nigger fall like a tree?" had echoed in his ears as he'd watched Sofronia try to shake her mother awake. The tears streaming down both of their faces had formed a single pool of moisture between them as they'd hugged each other tightly, unable to comprehend their loss.

Ivan had taken a lot of hits to the head, but he had a feeling the memory of Sofie screaming, "It's my fault" as she was pulled away from him would never get jarred loose. Nor would the thing he'd been too stunned to respond. *No, it's mine.* He was old enough to know now that it had been an unluckily timed medical ailment, but he'd always wondered if Sofie had allowed herself forgiveness. Seeing how tight and withdrawn she was now, compared to the rambunctious girl he'd known—he didn't think it was only adulthood that had made Sofie a dormouse.

Ivan took a quick shower and padded through the living room past his father, who was curled up on the old couch that had become his second bed over the last two years. Ivan knew that if he bothered to look down, he would see the photo album beside him.

Each night that Ivan found his father in this misery, he wanted to break the world. Leo Friedman wasn't an expressive man, but he'd loved his wife and missed her like hell, so much so that he could neither sleep in their marriage bed or dispose of it. Ivan had been by his father's side through the ritual stages of mourning—*aninut*, *shiva*, *shloshim*—but that hadn't released his dad from the grief that was always with him. He put on a good face at the synagogue and community events, but Ivan saw the toll the loss had taken on him. He was like a man whose shadow had been ripped away from him; every time he stepped out of the darkness and into the light, he need only look down to remember what he'd lost.

Ivan draped a crocheted blanket over him, then slid off the yarmulke that was being crushed against the arm of the sofa to reveal his father's thinning pate. His mother hadn't had any hair by the end of the cancer treatments, and her head had been smooth under his palm that last day. Ivan wanted to touch the vulnerable spot of scalp showing through, to give comfort where he could, but that would wake his father. These days they got along much better when one of them was sleeping.

He threw his gym bag over his shoulder as he stepped out into the still-dark morning and hopped onto his bike—not the Ducati Bronco he dreamed of owning, but a simple Schwinn. His dad needed the '54 Skylark they shared to get to his small watch repair shop in Richmond.

Ivan breathed in deeply as he propelled himself through the cool early morning air toward his boxing gym; the black gym on the edge of town, not the country club where the white boxers trained.

Jack's Gym had produced several champions, and even some guys who were working the circuit now. Ivan told himself he would've chosen Jack's anyway, even if he hadn't been banned from the country club. He hoped he would've, at least. It had been his home away from home since Miss Delia died, and he begged his mother not to force another nanny on him. He'd only been months away from becoming bar mitzvah, and had convinced his mother that he needed to put away childish things. He thought she'd caved so easily only because she missed Miss Delia too. "Delia, *zikhronah livrakha*. It's not as if I'll find anyone else who can make shlishkes as well as I can," she'd said with a shrug. It might have seemed cold to an onlooker, but coming from his mother that had been the highest compliment.

He pulled a key out from under a rubber tire near the door and let himself into the musty gym. The scents of sweat and sawdust made him feel more at home than the antiseptic smell of his house; his father had become troublingly obsessed with cleanliness after his mother's passing, spending hours at a time scrubbing the floors and counters.

Big Jack was there before him, as usual. The man was going on sixty-five and still strong and spry. Jack was working the heavy bag hard, which meant there was something on his mind.

"Did Loretta give you cold grits for breakfast again?" Ivan asked, hoping to pull a smile from the man.

"Loretta's cold grits are still better than anything you'll ever eat in your sorry life," Jack said. He kept punching. "Look at that paper over there."

Jack flicked his head in the direction of a table where a newspaper lay folded and a cup of coffee stood cold. Ivan picked up the crinkled mess, already knowing what type of image would greet him. A group of whites, hundreds of them at least, surrounding a Greyhound bus. A smaller image below showed a beaten man with blood streaming down his face being given water by what appeared to be a bystander. Ivan shuddered. The hatred in the eyes of the men surrounding the bus was chilling. Was this what had driven his parents from Budapest years before he was born? This undiluted disgust that could drive you to harm your fellow man simply for existing?

"These kids out there, your age or younger even, riding them buses and trying to make a change." Jack punched the bag hard, a blow that would have knocked a grown man out cold. "All that hope and idealism and those people said, 'We're gonna beat that hope right out of you.'"

Ivan taped his hands as his mentor punched and punched, letting the man work out his frustration. He flexed his hands, testing the give at his knuckles, and then walked over and held the bag still, absorbing the impact of Jack's last couple of punches. Jack breathed heavily, sweat coursing through the few wrinkles that showed his age, then rested his head against the bag.

"You know I'm not from these parts originally," he said. "My family is from Texas. Every year we had this Juneteenth celebration, and my grandpa would tell the story from when he was a boy. He saw the Union soldiers ride up with his own eyes and heard with his own ears when they let his people know they were free, that they had been for months, even though the slave masters had denied them that truth. That's kinda what this feels like. Like we still toiling, waiting for the *real* freedom to set in."

Jack looked up at him, despair in his eyes, and it dawned on Ivan that his friend was old. An old man in a state where slavery wasn't that distant a memory. Jack would tell anyone he'd lived a good life, doing what he loved, but Ivan knew there were stories that only came out after a drink or two. Stories about men with white hoods. Brightly burning crosses. Cars driving slowly through black neighborhoods while husbands and sons stood tensed on the porch with guns locked and loaded.

Jack sighed. "My grandkids are just getting old enough to understand the world. I hoped…I hoped life would be different for them."

Ivan hated seeing the way Jack's shoulders hunched in defeat. The man was a heavyweight champion, but he was buckling under the weight of the world.

"I went to a nonviolent resistance meeting last night," Ivan said. He didn't want a pat on the back, only to let Jack know where he stood.

Jack stared at Ivan for a long time and then laughed, a hacking laugh that might have sounded like respiratory distress to anyone who didn't know him. "Boy, you love throwing a punch more than any other boxer in here. What you doing with them Gandhi wannabes?"

"I do love it. I'm good at it, too," Ivan said as he took control of the heavy bag, warming up with quick, light blows. "But you know what I'm even better at? Taking a punch." He stopped his warm up and let the bag swing back and hit him. "If someone needs to take a beating for the cause, you can't do better than this ugly mug."

He thought of Sofie stepping in front of the group of boys all those years ago. There had been no fear in her despite being outnumbered and knowing society was on the boys' side no matter what—even children knew that fact. She'd been damned brave, and she'd done it for him.

Jack raised his brows, the question rippling in furrows that went right up his bald head. "Any not-ugly mug in particular you hoping to keep safe?"

Ivan sometimes forgot how well the man knew him.

"No way, Jack. I'm doing this because it's what's right. You don't join the Civil Rights movement for a woman. Come on." Ivan flung the bag Jack's way. Jack dodged it like a pro and continued scrutinizing him.

"No, but ain't nothing wrong with a bonus, like the prize in your Cracker Jacks. Besides, you ain't foolin' anyone with that dopey smile."

Ivan chuckled and allowed himself a moment of just being a guy who was really digging a girl. There was no way anything would come of it, but getting to see Sofie wasn't a chance he'd turn down.

"All right, enough of that, Romeo," Jack said. "You have a prizefight a week from now. This nonviolence stuff is well and good, but in here? There's only one thing I need from you, and ain't nothing peaceful about it."

chapter four

After studying for her upcoming final exams, Sofie had prepared her father's favorite dinner: meatloaf with mashed potatoes. A pitcher of sweet tea sat sweating on the table, and she absently drew a finger through the moisture accumulating on the wood surface as she created a list of her next moves in her head.

1.) Wait for Daddy to settle down at the table and talk about his day.

2.) Tell him how well studying for finals is going and mention you'll probably make the Dean's List again.

3.) Casually mention you'll be volunteering with an association a few nights this week.

4.) Dodge all questions about what, exactly, the association does.

5.) Pray he doesn't find out the truth, then pray for forgiveness for lying to begin with.

She left off number six, "Try not to stare at Ivan too much when you see him tomorrow," because it was probably not doable, and she hated listing actions that couldn't be checked off as completed. She'd been unable to stop thinking of him since the night before, even though she knew better. Having impure thoughts about a white man was bad enough, but one who wasn't even Christian was a definite no-no. She'd had a crush on him as a little girl, but that was different. He'd been the only boy who laughed at her jokes and refused to make fun of her frizzy hair. They'd spent hours creating fantastical worlds together where they were both brave and strong, where people couldn't hurt them just because of what they looked like, in Sofie's case, or what God they worshiped, in Ivan's. Their imaginary adventures had been brought to an abrupt halt, but Sofie's soft spot for him had apparently remained.

The shuffle of shoes against hard wood warned Sofie of her father's arrival; she stopped slouching in her seat and stood with her back straight and a bright smile on her face.

"Ready for dinner, Daddy?" she called out. She got no reply.

Mr. Wallis walked into the room with his hands linked behind his back and his head bowed. She remembered a time when he used to come into the kitchen with a smile, reaching for her mama with love in his eyes. Those days were long gone. Sofie stiffened in her seat, feeling the anxiety and anger emanating from her father fill the room like fumes that threatened to choke the bravery out of her. He was in a mood, and because he was in a mood her plan to ask permission would have to wait.

She took their plates from the stove, where she'd left them to warm. "I made your favorite. I think I've got Mama's recipe down pat now."

He looked up at her, and a familiar disappointment was etched deeply in his face, like ruts on a well-used road. "You planning on telling me what you were doing at that agitator meeting last night, or you just gonna sit here and talk to me like I'm stupid? Like you did last night when you lied and said you were meeting Henrietta?" His voice was so cold that she wanted to wrap her arms around herself in the warmth of a Southern spring night.

"Daddy, I can explain—"

"Sister Pierce told me she saw you in front of the community center, and that you were fraternizing with a white boy to boot. She said he looked quite familiar with you." He shook his head. "You're the first Wallis to go to college, and I was so proud of that. Now I have to wonder what it is you're really doing when you say you're in class or studying with friends."

Sofie hadn't eaten yet, and she was glad of it because her stomach gave a vicious twist. Nausea rolled through her at the anger in his words. She'd been caught in a lie, but he was also implying something about her that no father should imply about his daughter. His ideas about how an unmarried woman should and shouldn't interact with a man were old-fashioned, to put it kindly, but for him to treat her like a brazen hussy without giving her the benefit of the doubt…

All of her etiquette lessons and decorum fled her as disbelief hightailed it out of there to make room for anger. Sofie suddenly found she was standing, looking down at her father as he glared at her, waiting for his answer.

"All of these years I've been nothing but a good daught—" She choked on the word and swiped at a hot tear that slipped down her cheek. "A good daughter. I've done everything you asked of me, been your perfect little princess. And all it takes is one report from Mrs. Pierce and you're ready to call me a jezebel? Just like that?"

Her father picked up his fork and stabbed it into his meatloaf. "You didn't answer my question."

Sofie had thought she'd known loneliness before, but she'd been wrong. Loneliness was the one man who was supposed to protect and love you no matter what looking at you as if you were a mistake that needed fixing. Sofie had spent ten years suppressing so much of herself, just to please him; she'd thought one day she'd get it right, but the truth came to her like an icy deluge, shocking the warmth out of her. She could never be the daughter he wanted, not unless she found some way to make it so that Mama never died. Her hands were trembling fists at her side as she shook her head. "I was with Henrietta, *and* I was at the meeting."

"You admit you lied to me, then?"

"I didn't lie. I just didn't tell you the whole truth. And that's because I knew that you'd overreact like this instead of asking me why I wanted to volunteer or what I hoped to achieve." The anger was building in her; her voice shook from trying to contain her betrayal. "I was planning to ask your permission to participate, but I was a fool to think you'd care about what I want or need. All you've been after since Mama died was a perfect little girl who looked and talked and walked exactly as you liked. You should have just gotten yourself a porcelain doll because that's what you need more than a daughter."

"How dare you backtalk me?" His fist slammed on the table, making the silverware jump. "I've given you everything a girl could want, and all I've asked for in return was respect."

"What do I want, Daddy? Tell me. Because all you've given me is a list of ways in which I shouldn't embarrass you, and that's a poor excuse for a gift." She stared at him, fists balled at her sides.

Her father didn't answer, he simply pushed his plate away and left the room, as if she weren't significant enough to argue with. Sofie stood staring after him for a moment, but the creaking of the floorboards above her meant he was in his room, gone to bed for the night.

Her body moved on autopilot—she wrapped up their uneaten food, washed the dishes, cleaned up the crumbs. The same things she did every night. Only she had never argued with her father like this before—not out loud, at least. When he would explain the things she did wrong and how she should fix them, she'd always nodded and apologized. That was her burden to bear for dragging Mama into that fatal melee; submission was her penance, and she'd always paid it gladly. Tonight had been different in so many ways, though. She didn't want to apologize; in fact, she was surer than ever that joining the nonviolent movement was the right choice. She hated the lingering discord, but she hated more that her father could so easily find a reason to doubt her.

Sofie thought of the way Ivan had said, "You look the same." He was talking about the little girl that her father had called unkempt and unruly, but he said it like it was something good. She had the oddest urge to talk to him, to ask if his parents made him feel like he was only worthwhile if he did exactly as they said. But that was foolish. Ivan wasn't a friend she could call for support; he was nothing but a memory. And if she were smart, things would stay that way.

She was courting enough trouble as it were, Sofie thought as she carried her weary body to bed. Thinking of calling Ivan Friedman, or doing anything else with him, simply wasn't an option.

chapter five

Ivan had severely miscalculated how suddenly having Sofie in his life would affect him. He'd thought that being a grown man would've cured him of the ridiculous tightness in his stomach that used to strike whenever he thought of her. He'd thought he could keep his fantasies of how her curves would feel under his palms confined to his dreams.

But even now, as he sat squeezed into a too-small desk at the front of the room while fellow committee members berated him on everything from his looks to his heritage, all of his focus was on her. She was at the back of the room filing papers, making lists and putting things in order. That wasn't surprising—he remembered how she was always so careful to keep the kosher utensils from the non-kosher when she helped Miss Delia with the dishes like it was a challenge instead of a chore. Her gaze often wandered to the fracas at the front of the room. She'd caught him watching her more than once, looking away immediately every time. But he saw the way her hands clutched a pile of papers extra tightly, how she awkwardly knocked a box of pencils off the edge of the desk. He almost groaned when she went to her hands and knees, her dress tightening around her bosom and her full skirt revealing the delicate skin at the back of her knees. He wanted to run his tongue over that spot, but apparently

Sofie was a good girl now, and good girls didn't do those kinds of things.

"This guy seems pretty immovable," David said to the man helping him run the training, speaking as if Ivan weren't sitting right there. "But can we risk someone who beats people up for the joy of it?"

Two skeptical faces looked down at him.

"Hey, cool it with that kind of talk. Boxing is a beautiful sport; it's more than beating people up. That's not to say it doesn't require a certain affinity for violence," Ivan said. He cracked his knuckles and then flashed a smile at David. He wanted to look at Sofie but wasn't quite ready to see the disapproving expression that likely marred her face. "But the ability to dole out pain is also the ability to accept it. How many of you have ever taken a hit? Do you know how to block—not attack—how to contort your body to lessen the pain of a blow? How to take the violence that's being done to you and accept it as an inevitability? I can show you those things if you want."

Ivan didn't know what David was thinking. He might not like the idea of a random guy, and a white one at that, strolling in and presuming to exert any kind of authority. It would be the same as the Christians who sometimes showed up at his father's temple to tell the congregation about the New Testament and how gee-golly great it was, as if his people just hadn't thought to read past Deuteronomy.

David's eyes were narrowed in contemplation. "That could be useful to us. We'll see how the rest of the training goes. Sofie, come here. Switch with Lemuel. Lem, you're good for the sit-in. Remember to practice the meditation, deep breathing, and to reread from the selected texts beforehand."

Ivan tensed in his seat. He didn't know what David was up to or why he was calling Sofie to take part in this ugliness, but he didn't like it.

Breathe in, breathe out. He drew on his years of training and didn't let the way Sofie's hips swayed as she approached the desk, or the sweet vanilla scent of her as she passed in front of him, distract him.

Their gazes clashed again as she sat down, and Ivan felt a disconcerting sensation, similar to when an opponent had him against the ropes with no defenses. Everything about her was perfect—too perfect. Her pastel green dress, handmade so that it hugged every curve just right but didn't offer up everything on a platter. There was a series of tiny buttons down the sides of her dress; he doubted she knew what an enticement something so prim could be.

She was stiff in the seat beside him, and now that she was next to him she wouldn't look his way. Her back was straight, shoulders pushed back, and every strand of her hair was pomaded down and pulled into a tight bun. He wanted to reach over, undo those damned buttons, and maybe see what was keeping those stockings up beneath her skirt if not magic. He wanted all of that, but more, he wanted her to ask him to do it.

Sofie glanced at him warily, and Ivan hoped his face didn't project the lecherous path his thoughts were taking. There was a flushed look about her, same as the other night. She hadn't known who he was, but she had stared at him all night just the same. She wasn't the first woman who'd looked at him that way, but she was the only one who made it seem like she was breaking some rule by doing so. Ivan wasn't one for following the rules, and if she needed some guidance in that department, he'd be happy to help.

Henrietta rushed over. "This might be too much for her, David. I can do it if you want."

"Honey, you know Sofie isn't the kind of person to fight back. She'll be fine." David's words were hugely insulting, but for some reason he seemed to think he was being complimentary.

"You sure you talking about the same person, David? The Sofronia I knew had the quickest temper this side of the Mississippi," Ivan said. He was just joking, but she glared at him.

"The Sofronia you knew doesn't exist anymore," she said. Her voice was sweet, but only to cover the tartness of her words, like the candies he used to get by the bag from the five and dime. "And it's Sofie now. Sofie is nice, kind, quiet, and the last person to go around stirring up trouble."

Funnily enough, the bitterness underlying Sofie's words sounded a lot like Sofronia to him.

"I've been taking a physics class at college," Ivan said, leaning closer to her because his body didn't seem to want to do anything else. "My professor says that nothing can just stop existing. Energy can only change form. Maybe old Sofronia isn't down for the count just yet."

She crossed her arms and looked up at David. "Can we get on with this? My father is expecting me home soon." Ivan wondered why the mention of her father made her frown deepen. But training was back in session, and as much as he wished it were otherwise, he wasn't someone she would confide in.

David pressed up close behind them so that his thighs were touching both of them. "What do we got here? A nigger lover, boys."

The words scalded through Ivan. He knew this was fake. He knew there was no way that David was being malicious, but his jaw still clenched hard.

"Seems like this fool don't know that black pussy is only for getting your dick wet, not gallivanting around the streets with. You from up north? Yeah, that's it. Maybe you're a Yankee kike who thinks he's gonna change things down here."

Anger was coursing through him, but he didn't turn and pop David in the face like his instincts spurred him to. There was a lot of waiting in boxing if you were fighting someone good, and he'd wait out this barrage like he always did, except David wouldn't be sprawled on the floor afterward.

He glanced at Sofie, expecting to see her teary-eyed or hunched over, but when her dark eyes turned up to his they were rich with suppressed emotions. She didn't tremble, or acknowledge how everyone was hovering, waiting to pull her out of the scene in case it got too much for her. "Did you know that a teenage girl lost her baby last week?" she said calmly to Ivan, ignoring their fellow volunteers, who had now begun shoving them. Ivan shook his head. "She lived in my neighborhood and went to my church. The last time I saw her she was telling me how the sickness hit her at any time, not just morning, and could get so bad she couldn't stand. One day last week, she took a seat at the front of the bus."

Ivan didn't want to hear the rest of this, but Sofie seemed to be steeling herself with the story.

"I went and visited her today. She wasn't trying to be an activist—she just didn't want to vomit and she couldn't hardly move once she sat down. A police officer shoved her off the bus, beat her, and then said she was resisting. They didn't take her to the hospital when she said she couldn't feel her baby kicking anymore."

There was a silence as Sofie's hard gaze left Ivan's face and she looked at the other volunteers. "Now all I can think about is how a black baby can be killed just to ensure that a white person gets a seat. And it makes me angry. It makes me wish I had the power to set this world ablaze, but, lucky for some people, I don't. So nothing anyone screams at me is worse than the knowledge that Patty's baby was alive and now it's dead. A beating won't make me forget that every day of my life I have to defer to someone else just because I have more melanin. I can go to a sit-in and take whatever these people dish out, but don't make the mistake of thinking I'll do it because I'm nice."

There was something about the way the word *nice* scraped out of her throat that made the hairs on Ivan's neck stand on end. She had obviously shocked the people around her, the people who were supposed to know her best, but the only thing that surprised him was that she'd waited this long to let it all hang out.

"Wait, are you saying you want to do the sit-in, Sofie?" Henrietta clasped her hands together as if she was speaking to a child. "What will your father say?"

"And what if you get hurt?" David asked.

"What if I do?" Sofie asked. "It's the chance we all take. You just sent me up here because you thought it would be funny. Because I'm so *sweet*." She laughed bitterly then, and if anyone had been under that impression, they were surely changing their minds now. "The bottom line is I'm one of the best-qualified people to do this sit-in. I'm young, photogenic, and I've been quietly suffering fools for most of my life. I can do this."

"Girl, I just knew there was more to you than that Miss Prim and Proper," Henrietta said with a relieved sigh. "Sometimes you just got that little extra edge in your voice, and I knew it couldn't be gas all the time."

When Sofie's eyes flashed back to Ivan, they were sparkling with challenge.

The door to the common room flew in and a young man, lanky and high yellow, called out, "Come see the news. Come! It's horrible."

The scenes on the small black-and-white television looked like something out of a war film. The camera panned over a mob of white men surrounding an interstate bus, ravening as they broke out windows with pipes and rocks and attacked the people inside. On the outskirts of the crowd, women dressed in skirts and dresses cheered them on, their faces contorted into masks of hatred. Some of them cradled infants in their arms. A shell-shocked news reporter tried to explain what was happening behind him. "They say that they're going to burn them alive in the bus. Folks at home, remember that these are six members of a nonviolent protest group and there are innocent passengers who have nothing to do with the protest." A man ran by and shoved the reporter, and then there was a loud whoosh, like the sound of a lit matchmaking contact with the gas from a stovetop burner. There were even more screams as flames shot out of the back of the bus.

All of the air seemed to disappear from the room around them as they surrounded the small television. Ivan heard an ugly sound from next to him and saw that Lemuel, the man he had been practicing with, was fighting against the sobs rising up in his throat. He realized that the black students had moved together unconsciously, leaving a buffer zone between him and them. Between the person who looked like the attackers on television and those who looked like most of the protestors being beaten. Sofie still stood beside him. Her expression was unreadable. She didn't cry like the man on the other side of him, but there was something infinitely sadder in the way she regarded the screen. He thought of how he'd felt when shown pictures of emaciated concentration camp survivors, knowing they had committed the same crime as him: being born Jewish. When it came to the pictures of the piles of bodies, he'd always closed his eyes, afraid of seeing some familiar feature that revealed his grandparents or his aunt Ilona or any of the other Friedmans who hadn't escaped the machinations of the Third Reich. Seeing those images in black and white, and in the black ink tattooed on some of the worshipers at synagogue, had made everything real in a way his imagination could not.

"They're not allowing the Riders to exit." The reporter talked slowly as if considering whether each word could actually be true whether his eyes were deceiving him. Ivan felt something wrap around his arm—Sofie's hands had clasped his biceps, seemingly just to hold herself up. They all stared on as the fire engulfed the bus. Another explosion sounded and the mob cleared from around the bus, allowing the passengers to escape.

"Shit." Ivan didn't know who said it. It could have been him. The moment of elation for the people escaping was short-lived as the mob closed around them and began beating and kicking and tearing; they were out for blood, and they got it. The crowd surrounded a white man with thick horn-rimmed glasses as he stumbled off the bus coughing; a man teed up with a metal pipe like he was at baseball practice and swung at his face, laughing as the man with glasses crumpled to the ground. As if on signal, the police finally moved in.

David shut the television off. His shoulders heaved, and for a moment Ivan thought he was preparing some kind of rousing battle cry. Instead, his voice was broken when he turned to the other students and spoke. "This is what we are fighting against, brothers and sisters. Do you understand that these people see us as subhuman? Or worse: humans who might be just as good as them." He glanced at Ivan. "They'll see you as a race traitor. They'll want to give it to you good."

"Consider me Judas, then," Ivan said. "I've heard all the stories of how my people knew Kristallnacht and the purges and something even worse were coming, but everyone hoped it could be avoided somehow. Hope alone can't change things in this country. You're trying to do that, and I intend to help."

"I'm still in," Sofie said. "I imagine that after seeing that, you're going to have a lot more volunteers."

"And a lot more enemies," Henrietta added.

"Do not fear or be dismayed because of this great multitude, for the battle is not yours but God's," David said. His voice was strong again, and the vehemence of it raised goosebumps on Ivan's arms despite his neutrality when it came to religion. "Everybody join hands," David said, and the students obeyed. "Let's sing, together, and know that just as our voices are joined, our will shall be joined, too."

Sofie's hand was warm in Ivan's as the song began, but her voice was low as if she had muted herself. He wanted to lean down to hear her, but just being able to touch her was enough. "Let the circle, be unbroken, by and by, by and by."

Ivan hadn't known what he'd expected when he volunteered, but as the words of his new compatriots mingled with his own deep voice, he was reminded of the sense of connection and unity he only experienced on the high holy days or on those trips to synagogue that had grown few and far between.

"We'll meet here again tomorrow night," David said. He pulled Henrietta close, and they swayed there, supporting each other. "Would you mind leading a session at tomorrow night's meeting?" David asked. "I would appreciate it. Fisticuffs aren't my forte."

Ivan nodded. The pride that surged through him could have been considered a sin, but then again even the Talmud conceded that a scholar must possess at least an eighth of an eighth of pride in his studies. It wasn't often that people looked at what he had spent years studying, as diligently as any Torah scholar, as something useful to the greater good. His own father compared him to a common thug, as if the Jewish boxers who'd dominated the sport for years had meant nothing. But now Ivan had a chance to help people, and one person in particular.

Sofie hugged her arms around herself, her earlier vim and vigor gone. "I—I can't come tomorrow night. I have to have dinner with my father. He's not happy about me coming here and…" She shrugged, and her full mouth compressed into a thin line as she held back some emotion. Ivan didn't know what words she struggled for in trying to describe what was happening with her father, only that he felt them, too.

"You busy in the afternoon?" he asked her.

She regarded him suspiciously, and Ivan hated that she didn't trust him, but loved that she was smart enough not to.

"I have a class in the morning, but I'm free in the afternoon. Why?"

"Because if what we just saw is any indication of how bad things can go, you're going to have to learn how to take a hit." He looked at the other students. "And if you can't come tomorrow night, you'll be missing some important information."

He knew that last line was a little manipulative. The Sofronia he'd known hated missing out on anything, and hated not having all the information available to her. She'd even refused to read their children's books out of order because she wanted to know what happen in the rest of the series.

"Do you want to swing by my place after your class? Or would you prefer I come to you?" He tried to make the interaction as normal as possible, like it made complete sense for the two of them to be alone.

"I'm not sure about being alone in a house with you," she said.

Ivan ran a hand through his hair. "I guess I can pretend to attack you outside and we can see how that goes."

"The same way it always goes when a white man attacks a black woman," she said, a hand dropping onto her hip. "No one would do anything to help me and you could go on about your day afterward."

Ivan felt her words like a hard right to the jaw. He knew that the bond they shared was based on childhood friendship, and that many things had happened to them both in the intervening time. But for her to lump him in with *them*, with men who would hurt her because they could, was a low blow. The fact that everyone around them was not pretending to be otherwise engaged meant they felt the sting of her words too.

"I'm sorry. That wasn't fair to you when you're just trying to help." Her lips pressed into a line. "Do you still live…" She paused and Ivan filled in the blank. *Where Miss Delia died?* "…at the same address?"

He nodded.

"I'll be there around three," she said. Ivan realized he had expected her to say no, and tried not to show how surprised he was by her response.

"I'll be waiting," he said.

chapter six

Dragging your feet wasn't very ladylike, but Sofie was second-guessing her decision as she walked down the tree-lined street leading up to the Friedmans' house. She didn't want to see Ivan and his mother and be reminded of all that she'd lost—and what more she might lose if her father continued to greet her with a stony silence.

She hated that a part of her was looking forward to being visiting the scene of the most awful moment of her life. She'd never returned after her mother's death; that meant she'd never gotten to taste Mrs. Friedman's delicious food again, or to tell her how Mama had loved the challenge of mastering the specialized cuisine.

She rang the bell, then adjusted the plate of cookies she had baked the night before when thoughts of Ivan and sit-ins and bloodied students had stolen her sleep. She often turned to the comfort of her mother's recipe box when she was unsettled. She knew it was strange, but the notes were so detailed she felt like her mother had channeled some of herself into those family secrets, as if she had known that she wouldn't be around to show Sofie just how long to simmer the collards or how much sugar she meant by "to taste." Sofie sometimes pretended her Mama was with her as she whisked and chopped and folded, only it didn't always feel like pretend.

Ivan pulled the door open then, and the smile Sofie had plastered on crumbled away. He stood before her freshly showered and smelling of ninety-nine point forty-four percent pure goodness. His hair was still wet, his face freshly shaved. That was all well and good, but her gaze was drawn to his body: the ropy muscles of his arms, the broad chest—Sofie's lingering sense of decorum didn't allow her to look any further down than that.

"Hey! Come on in." He stood aside, and she was forced to pass close to the warmth that radiated off him. She didn't know why he was affecting her this way. She'd been close to him more than once already, but there had been other people around before. The delicious smell of onions and garlic was emanating from the kitchen, and she realized it was Friday. His mother was probably making the stew for Shabbos. His mother or whomever they had hired in place of hers. Sofie felt a little bit nauseated at the thought of stepping into the kitchen and seeing another black woman working there, as if her mother were easily replaceable.

"I made some cookies," she said. "Is your mother in the kitchen? I can bring them in to her."

The door slammed shut and the effortless sex appeal Ivan had exuded shifted as he hunched in on himself. He cleared his throat. "Mom died two years ago. Cancer."

"Oh! Oh." Tears pressed at her eyes suddenly. She hadn't seen Mrs. Friedman in years but the news still hurt. Another part of her childhood, gone. Ivan had been there for her in those awful moments when she'd lost her own mother. Who had been there for him?

She lifted a hand, but it hung in the air between them, not quite able to span the distance. "I'm so sorry. I didn't know."

He nodded, then lifted the plate of cookies from her other hand and walked toward the kitchen. She followed behind him, searching for something to say to make up for her atrocious error. She was surprised to see him place the cookies on the table, pick up a large knife, and begin chopping potatoes. Her arrival had obviously interrupted him. "Sorry. I just need to throw this stuff into the slow cooker. Dad still hasn't learned how to make cholent, and if I don't cook it, he just won't eat tomorrow."

She pulled up a seat at the kitchen island, warding off memories of so many years before. It was strange to remember the young, frail Ivan who would sit next to her at this very counter and listen to her mother's stories as she looked at him before her, all grown up and cooking for the family himself. "That's nice of you," she said. "Sometimes I think the same thing about my father. I try to make something good most nights. Otherwise, he would just survive on TV Dinners."

Ivan chuckled, then reached behind him with the knife and used it to pull open the freezer, which was stuffed to the gills with the distinctive frozen meals. Sofie gave a bittersweet laugh.

"Women from our synagogue cook extra food and bring him their 'leftovers,' but he hates eating that. He says it makes him feel ungrateful when he thinks their food isn't as good as my mom's." Ivan dumped the barley, potatoes, and beans into the slow cooker, then took the onions off the stove and scraped them in as well. "The only person who could ever match Mom in the kitchen was Miss Delia. She never stopped talking about her, you know. Even on her death bed she said, 'If Delia were here she could show these di skeynes how to make some real matzah ball soup!'"

Sofie smiled. She remembered how hard Mrs. Friedman had been on her mother during the first few weeks. Mama came home complaining about the woman every night. But when Mama had shown her she was no one's fool in the kitchen, they'd developed a type of friendship. As much friendship as could exist between a servant and the woman she worked for.

Ivan washed his hands and wiped them off on his jeans. "Okay, you ready to get to it?"

Sofie nodded, and felt the oddest trembling in her stomach as he approached her. She didn't think she'd ever paid much attention to the way a man walked before, but she watched the play of muscle as he took each step and how his arms swung in a way that projected an unconscious self-confidence. He gave her his chip-toothed grin as he stopped in front of her and nodded in the direction of her hands. "You should take those off. I wouldn't want to be responsible for sullying your gloves."

"They'll likely be destroyed at a real sit-in," she said.

He took her hand from where it rested on the counter and undid the small button at the base of her glove, and it was if that one flick of his finger released a torrent of tingling heat that spread from her wrist to her arm and through the rest of her body. "I can only be responsible for my own actions," he said. "And I don't want to be the man who shredded these dainty little things." He pinched the fingertip of the glove and gave it a tug, and Sofie felt the responding pull between her thighs.

She should have grabbed her hand away from him then, as soon as that first bolt of pleasure went through her, but she simply stared up at him with wide eyes as he gave four more swift, gentle pulls and freed her hand from its encasement. He took the other hand, moving one step forward as he did, so that now the roughness of his denim pants rubbed against her knee as he worked.

Sofie knew he could see her hand shaking, and her chest rising and falling heavily, and the way her knees were pressed together. She was embarrassed, but that didn't mean she wasn't disappointed too when he pulled her second glove off the final digit, her pinky, and laid it down besides its mate.

She forced herself to look up at him, and was happy to see that his cheeks were flushed beneath his fading bruises. Ivan may have been cool now, but not so cool that she didn't affect him, too. "Okay, we should go into the living room."

She stood on wobbly legs and clicked after him across the tiled kitchen floor. "Should I take off my shoes, too?" she asked. It was a brazen thing to ask, but her fingers were still tingling from his touch.

Ivan stopped and looked back over his shoulder. His gaze fixed on her pointy black leather heels, then up her stocking leg until her skirt obstructed his view. His voice was low and his gaze intense when he answered, and his words made her throat go dry.

"Leave your heels on."

chapter seven

Half an hour later, they sat stiffly beside each other on the couch.

"It's okay. I'm sure it happens to the best of boxers," she said. Mortification clenched him by the back of the neck.

He hadn't thought through the most important part of the training: pretending to hit her. He couldn't do it. He couldn't even bring himself to throw a fake, loose-fisted punch that he knew would miss her by a mile. Sofie had stood in front of him, eyes wide and lovely, lips soft and distracting, and his fists had hung limply at his side. And now they sat in awkward silence.

"This is ridiculous," Ivan said. He grabbed Sofie's hand and stood, pulling her up after him. When he turned she was giving him that ingénue look again, the one he usually only saw on the screen at the Saturday matinee. In the films, a look like that was an invitation, but he doubted Sofronia was offering him any such thing. He placed his hands on her shoulders. "First things first: you need to relax." He gave her a gentle shake to loosen her muscles, which had tensed up as soon as he laid his hands on her. "You need to be a little soft to take a hit; leave a little give so the impact won't hurt as much."

He wished he had phrased it differently—thinking of the soft parts of Sofie was making him uncomfortably hard, and that wasn't what this afternoon was supposed to be about.

She nodded, but the relaxation didn't come. Instead, she started to tremble a little beneath his palms and her gaze dropped to the floor.

"No." Ivan slid his fingers under her chin and lifted her head. He didn't miss that her skin was smooth beneath his fingertips. "Maintain eye contact. If someone is about to hit you, you want to see it coming so you can act accordingly."

"Okay." She locked her gaze on his, and his stomach executed an unfamiliar twisting maneuver. It was a funny thing to look into a woman's eyes like this. Intimate encounters were nothing new for him; ladies liked a guy who could hit and punch and dominate in the ring. Caveman attraction, and all that jazz. But no one had ever looked at him the way Sofie did, that's for sure. Her eyes were full of contradictions: fear and longing, humor and distaste. Maybe he'd been wrong about the invitation. Maybe she was just waiting for his RSVP, like any proper lady would. Ivan's groin tightened at the thought and wisps of desire feathered down his spine.

He slid one hand over the crisp fabric that nipped in at her shoulder and then his palm was on smooth, warm skin. He cradled the back of her neck, and the way the curls at her nape tickled his palm was enough to make him want to pull the pins out of her bun and dive his fingers into the soft mass. Instead he exhaled slowly and continued his instruction. "You can be stiff here." He gave her neck a little squeeze. "And tuck in your chin. Yeah, like that. That way your head won't snap back if you take one to the face." He didn't move his hand away; not just yet. Neither Jack nor any of the other boxers had ever touched him this gently during training, but this wasn't the gym. This was Sofie, for Pete's sake.

His other hand left her shoulder, ghosted past her breast, and rested on her stomach. "You should brace here, too, if someone hits you. That way the wind won't get knocked out of you. A blow to the diaphragm while your stomach is soft can make you feel like you're dying."

He felt like he was dying, all right. Sofie still had her eyes locked on his, and her tongue slicked nervously over her lips. Her skin had gone hot beneath the fabric of her dress, and he could feel the way her heart was racing just above where his hand rested.

Ivan didn't think. His fist tightened, twisting up the fabric under his hand and pulling Sofie two steps closer to him.

"Ivan." His name was almost a question. What was the right answer? Damned if he knew.

"Last thing: roll with the punches. When something comes at you, you have to roll with it. Go in the same direction to lessen the impact." His face was lowering as he spoke, his mouth on a slow collision course with hers. At the last minute, she turned her face to the side and back, leaving his mouth beside her ear. Disappointment rocked through him, but he said what any good trainer would say. "Good job. You're a fast learner."

Both of her hands came over his, pulling it closer to the soft curve of her belly. Her fingertips traced the indentations in his knuckles before she exhaled shakily and pushed his hand away. "You're wrinkling my dress," she whispered, then stepped back. "I should go."

He moved away from her and she turned and marched away, hips swaying as she balanced on those pointy heels. She grabbed her bag and trotted down the hall. "Thank you very much for the lesson!" she called over her shoulder.

Ivan stood staring long after the door slammed. Sofie had learned to take a hit, so why was he the one left feeling punch drunk? He bounded up the stairs to change into his gym clothes. Only a long round with the heavy bag, and maybe a sparring match, would be able to rid him of the foolish notion that Sofie could ever be his.

chapter eight

They want to stop the rides," Henrietta said when Sofie walked into the community center the following Monday. Sofie was supposed to be studying at the university, but she'd gotten off the bus early and come to the community center.

"Why," she asked.

"Did you see what happened in Birmingham?" Henrietta asked. Sofie shook her head. "After beating those people half to death at the bus depot, they wouldn't let them leave. They were trapped at the airport for hours with the same mob that attacked them because no flights would take them. It's a miracle they got out of there, but now they're not going to try to reach New Orleans."

Sofie's heart dropped. "But that means…"

"That means violence took the day," David said, rubbing the crease between his eyes. He was sprawled in his chair, looking as tired as Sofie had ever seen him. "It means people will think that the movement can be stopped by bats and pipes and heartlessness."

"Well, we have to do something," Sofie said. David and Henrietta looked at her warily. After all, it was an un-Sofie-like thing to say. Heck, she was wary of herself these days. But that fire in her chest was going again, and the idea that was forming in her mind made more and more sense.

"Like what?" Henrietta asked.

"I'm feeling a mite peckish. I think I might take a trip downtown and order myself a nice hamburger." Sofie pulled on her gloves and a memory flashed in her mind, of her and Ivan pretending to go into battle during one of their childhood games. Then the memory of him unbuttoning the very same gloves the day before. She'd been out with boys before, had kissed and fumbled and explored—even good girls did that. But the way Ivan touched her had seared into her. None of the other boys had ever made her feel like that, and that just added to her guilt, because none of them had looked like Ivan either.

What is wrong with me? She couldn't be entirely upset. Whatever this madness within her was, it was about to take her to the Special K diner, and that was exactly where she needed to be.

"Sofie, we aren't prepared," David said. "I know you're upset right now, but flying off the handle isn't going to change anything."

"No, it's not. But I'm tired of being afraid." The words came out almost a shout, and she calmed herself. David wasn't responsible for Jim Crow, or for the way her father tried to cut off everything he deemed bad about her, like eyes off a potato. "I'm tired of living like this," she said more calmly. "And I refuse to let any bigot in Richmond sit and pat himself on the back and think for *one minute* that people like us got put in their place. I'm going, David. I'm a grown woman and I don't need your permission to do as I wish."

That thought was a revelation to her. She hated that her father was mad, but she only needed his love, not his permission. If he would deny her the former, well, that said more about him than it ever would about her.

"Well, you do need one thing from me," David said.

"And what's that?" Henrietta asked, standing beside Sofie. Her friend had put on her Jackie Kennedy sunglasses, which meant she was ready for serious business.

David held up his key ring and jingled it. "A ride."

Hell and damnation," David said, as they walked into the popular Greek diner. Sofie knew he was more than nervous if he was getting biblical with his cursing.

Sofie noted with the bit of humor that was available through her fear that Elvis's "It's Now or Never" was playing on the jukebox when they walked in.

The place was packed, but they had just seen four men get up and leave the lunch counter from their perch outside. Purpose was the only thing that had carried Sofie in through the door after Henrietta, the support that kept her legs from wobbling and giving way as they approached the counter. The place was noisy, raucous, full of teenagers enjoying their weekend and families taking a break from a day of shopping downtown. The happy chatter got quieter as David took his seat. By the time Sofie dropped onto the round leather stool, a low, ugly murmur was going through the crowd, accentuated by the happy, tinkling piano of the Elvis song.

A man approached the counter, wiping his hands on his towel. Sofie's body stiffened, and then she heard Ivan's voice say "Relax," and she did that to the best of her ability. She expected the man to yell at them, to look at them with derision, but instead his eyes were filled with sadness. "Please don't do this. Not here," he said. His voice was heavily accented and shaking, but not with anger.

Once when she was a girl, a carnival had come through town; only after Sofie had been strapped into the tilt-o-whirl did she see that the operator was a boy not much older than her. The same deep, primordial terror that her life might, indeed, be over pressed down on her as she sat at the counter. She began relisting the rules of a sit-in over and over in her mind in order to calm herself.

1.) Behave in a friendly manner.

"Can we get three coffees, please, sir?" Henrietta asked sweetly.

"I can't," the man said. "You know I can't. Why you want to make my life hell?"

2.) Sit straight and always face the counter.

"Okay, we're just going to read here until you change your mind," David said with a smile. They remained silent then, each clutching a book they could use to study for finals. Sofie opened her book, but the words were so much gibberish, and she thought it would shake right out of her hands. She read the same line over and over because she didn't think she'd be able to turn the page.

"I can't let you stay," the man said. Sofie heard the scrape of chairs as patrons stood up. "They're gonna hurt me and they're gonna hurt you. I don't want things to be like this, but what can I do? I just came here a few years ago."

And you already have a diner because you have blue eyes and light skin and can pass for one of them, Sofie wanted to say. She knew the man was distraught, but that didn't change the fact that she would not stand up.

3.) Don't strike back if struck, or curse back if cursed upon.

"What do you niggers think you're doing?" a voice said from behind them. "This ain't Nashville." She could feel the people coming up behind her and realized this was one thing they hadn't practiced, this innate desire to turn and ward off a dangerous animal creeping up on you. The hairs stood up on the back of her neck, and when someone gripped her chair from behind, the word "Mama" was incomprehensibly heavy on her tongue. But her mother couldn't help her.

David had repeated a version of Psalm 118 to them as they approached the diner, and Sofie let those words fortify her. *The Lord is for us. We shall not fear. What can man do to us? The Lord is for us among those who help us; therefore, we shall look with satisfaction on those who hate us.*

A bulky frame brushed past her left side and slid into the seat, and Sofie tensed, then relaxed, preparing for a blow. "Can I get a milkshake?" a familiar voice asked. "I know things are a little hectic, but I've had a day. A malted would be perfect."

4) Don't laugh out.

The harried restaurant owner ignored Ivan and tried to calm the crowd that was getting more riled now that the interlopers at the counter were racially mixed.

Sofie inhaled the scent of Ivory soap and felt a bit of peace. Why was it that she had gone so long without Ivan in her life, but now, after just a few days, he could make her feel safe? It wasn't that he was a boxer; she didn't expect him to protect them from the men in the crowd, which was growing more agitated by the minute. He fortified something in her that David and Henrietta, her best friends, did not. She remembered Mrs. Friedman shaking her head at their games and asking her mother, "What is this saying they have here? Two peas in a pod? That's these two."

"You okay?" Ivan asked in a low tone. His seat creaked beneath his weight as he settled more solidly beside her.

6.) Don't hold conversations.

"Hush," she said under her breath. She kept her face toward her book, but beneath the counter, Ivan's knee pushed into hers, stopping her leg from shaking. He was giving her some of his strength. That was probably the least important thing happening in the Special K diner in that moment, but it felt like everything. When she glanced at him, he was pulling a newspaper from under his arm, whistling. He winked with his right eye, like he knew she was watching, and she turned back to her book.

"Think you're smart?" an ugly voice said, and the book was ripped out of her hands from behind. She heard the sounds of tearing behind her, and hated that something that could be used for knowledge was being destroyed, but there was nothing she could do. She folded her hands in front of her. Beside her she heard another ugly voice say, "You wanted a milkshake?" She knew it was a different man, but the hatred distorted their voices so they all sounded the same. Gales of laughter suddenly surrounded her, and she looked at Ivan. Chocolate milkshake dripped down his hair and onto his face, but his expression was serene.

There was more laughter, and then Henrietta yelped. Her precisely flat-ironed hair was now dripping with fountain soda. A shiver went through her, and then she threw her shoulders back and stared straight ahead.

A thickly accented voice rang out over the noise. "The diner is now closed, everybody out!" A much larger man, obviously the son of the owner, was standing by the door, directing people outside. "All of you out!"

Sofie sat still as people slapped at her chair on their way out. Finally there was the jingle of the bells over the door, and then silence. The son came over and slapped a hand on the counter. "You trying to ruin us? You know how much money we lost tonight? You get out, too."

Sofie wanted to apologize, but she refused. It was the animals who had attacked them and ruined the store who should apologize. Still, she couldn't stop the guilt that tugged at her heart when the older man emerged with a broom, eyes rimmed with red. "Enough, Constantine. They're doing what they have to, like I did what I had to in my day. You were born here, so you have no idea." The man sighed. "I understand, but…please leave now. I have a lot of cleaning to do."

Sofie saw David stand, and followed his lead. As they filed out, her stomach felt sour and her heart heavy. Had they accomplished anything, or would this count as another loss for the movement?

She didn't have time to think on it, because a glass bottle crashed at her feet, and then another.

"Run!" Henrietta screamed, and then they were off. Without thinking, her hand slipped into Ivan's and they careened through the midday crowd, pushing past amazed onlookers as angry shouts followed them down the street.

"This way." He pulled her into an alley between a pet shop and a pharmacist and kept running. He turned left and then right and then boosted her over a fence, something she hadn't done since her tomboy days.

Her stockings were ruined, her gloves were shredded, and her heart was beating out of her chest. What had she done? What had she gotten herself into?

There was a thud as Ivan landed in the small enclosure behind her. They both breathed heavily for a moment, but there were no pounding footsteps heading in their direction, no hoots and hollers from people who wanted to do them harm.

"Did they hurt you?" He stalked toward her with that intense gaze that made her feel like the center of his universe.

"No," she said. The word was barely out of her mouth when his mouth came down on hers and her mind went blank.

The man could kiss. Sofie had been kissed before and kissed well, but this was something entirely different. His lips were warm and smooth, and so, so soft. It evoked a sort of tenderness in her that a man so strong, who brawled with other men by choice, could have such sweet, soft lips. They rubbed over hers, tantalizing, before his tongue swept into her mouth. He tasted of the milkshake that had been tossed on him, and of peppermint candy.

Sofie knew she should pull away, but instead let him kiss her. Spirals of pleasures cycloned through her body, picking up the anger and fear and adrenalin surging through her and churning it all into lust. She didn't want to think of the men who hated her and the things they'd called her. She didn't want to feel that sick sadness anymore. In Ivan's arms, all of that faded away, leaving only pleasure. His large hands encircled her waist holding her in place as he kissed her senseless. One hand slid up her back, cradling her neck as he transferred his kisses from her mouth, to her jaw, to her neck.

Sofie touched her neck every day—bathing, applying perfume—but never had she known it could feel so damned good. The skin there seemed oversensitized, so that Ivan's every touch multiplied and raced off through her like the Pony Express, carrying messages of the pleasure to come to the further regions of her body.

The brush of his lips converted the fluttering in her belly into something warm and fluid as molasses that settled warmly between her legs. The scrape of his stubble made her rub her thighs together to assuage the need for touch. And then his teeth grazed her skin as his hand moved up to cup her breast, and she bucked in his arms at the jolt of it. His thumb ran over the pebbled nipple through the material of the dress, slowly caressing as his tongue circled around that wonderful spot where neck and shoulder met.

"Jesus," she moaned, the word the only thing that could convey what Ivan's mouth and hands were doing to her. The power and the glory, indeed.

"Wrong Jew," he said, and kissed her again.

Sofie faintly heard a tinkling noise that began to pull her back to reality, but the sound of the back door of a shop opening seemed to reach her in slow motion. She didn't push Ivan away until after she heard a man call out his name angrily, until after she heard the ugly word "schvartze," yet another derogatory term for her people, mixed in with an angry deluge of Yiddish. Ivan pulled away from her.

The magic of the moment disappeared and Sofie realized that they were standing behind a dumpster, like so much refuse. Shame flooded her when she saw the expression of disgust on the man's face, but even being caught red-handed like a back-alley hussy couldn't strip her of her manners.

"Nice to see you again, Mr. Friedman." She turned to Ivan, who looked like he had much more impolite things to say to his father. "I have to get home."

"I'll give you a ride," he said.

"Not in my car you won't." Mr. Friedman moved to block his path.

"I paid that car off with my own money. I'll never use it again after tonight, but I'll be damned if I let Sofie get hurt by the bigots who just chased us down." Ivan shook his head. "You're just as bad as them. Worse. You know what it is to be on the other side, you know what it is to be hated for no reason, and you still can't sympathize. You think they cared about the difference between a Sephardi and a schvartze in the camps?"

He walked around his father, as if he couldn't bear to be in his vicinity, and Sofie followed behind him. By the time she reached the car, she was shaking. She didn't know if it was anger or shock as the adrenalin left her.

"Sof."

She ignored his voice.

"Sofie. Please look at me."

She turned her head slowly. She wanted to hate him, as his father's ugly slur echoed in her head, but she also wanted to take out her handkerchief and wipe off his face. It seemed that when it came to Ivan, conflicting emotions were the rule and not the exception.

"You need to go home and clean up, and I need to go home and be told what an ungrateful child I am." She sighed, feeling a weariness that went deep into her bones.

"In that case, you should understand that fathers and their children often have differences of opinion."

"Difference of opinion?" She whirled, suddenly angry. "Your father thinks I'm a schvartze. A nigger."

He started the car. "And your father thinks Jews are cheap, hook-nosed bastards. At least, that's what he called my parents when he came to collect the last of your mother's things. 'Cheap, hook-nosed bastards who worked Delia to the grave,' but I might be paraphrasing. It was a long time ago."

Sofie sucked in a breath. All of the little asides her father had made over the years ran through her mind. How the mechanic tried to "Jew him down" instead of saying he haggled. How he'd always referred to the Friedmans as *those people.* "So, what? Is that supposed to excuse what your father said?" Sofie asked.

"Nope," Ivan replied, and his calm riled her all the more. "But it excuses us. I'm going to have words with my father later, but I won't be held responsible for his."

Sofie sat in her seat, feeling as if she were being torn in two. She had stood up for herself today, and she had been attacked for it, just like before. Ivan had been with her just as before, too. Sofie was waiting for the wrath of God to rain down on her now. Wasn't that what happened when she took a little something for herself? But the wrath of Mr. Friedman was nothing compared to what she'd been through. And Ivan was still beside her now, glancing at her with a warm seriousness as he navigated her home.

"Why did you kiss me?" she asked quietly. She couldn't control anything else in the world, despite how much she wanted to, but she could control what happened between them. A few days ago she wouldn't have even considered such a thing a possibility, but now she desperately wanted to hear his answer, and not only so she could discount it.

"Because you're beautiful. God, you're beautiful." The words rasped out of him like they were painful, and instead of fire in her chest, Sofie felt a cool fluttering sensation. "Because you're smart and sexy and strong as hell, and you've got everyone fooled but me. I see you in there behind the quiet voice and the pillbox hats, Sofronia. And I'm still here waiting."

Sofie opened her purse and pulled out a handkerchief. She reached out and gingerly wiped away at the milkshake that had spread over his face. It was the only thing she could think to do besides bend over and weep from the blow of such an unexpected kindness. It seemed the last years of her life had been a *Twilight Zone* episode in which she'd been stuck in someone else's life. She'd heard all about how wonderful Sofie was from behind the carefully constructed mask, which of course meant that her, the *real* her, was the opposite of wonderful. Didn't it? Ivan didn't seem to think so, and that affected her even more deeply than their kiss had.

His face was in profile to her as he drove, but she saw at least half of his smirk as she wiped the remains of the dessert drink from his hair.

"Searching for horns?" he asked, trying to make her laugh. It worked, even though something about the way he said it, with that half-quirked smile of his, made her stomach somersault too.

"Don't be silly, you don't have horns," she said, but she dropped the handkerchief and thrust her fingers into his thick hair anyway, the slide of it against her fingers a strange, smooth sensation. It was thick and curly, but in a different way from her own. She ran her fingernails over his scalp, and watched in amazement as he shivered.

"Why'd you check if you were so sure?" he asked when she pulled her hand away. His voice had the same joking tone, but was huskier now, activating something in Sofie that was receptive to this new octave that hinted at darkened bedrooms and the things that happened in them.

"Maybe I just wanted to touch you," she said, shocked that she had told him the God's honest truth. Henrietta would never let her live this down if she told her, and her father would about kill her if he found out. But something in Ivan crowded out what anyone else would think, and what the world could do to them.

She pulled her hand away as the car pulled to a stop in front of her house. She could see the light on in the living room and the shadowy form of her father through the curtains, and sighed.

Ivan's hand encircled her wrist as she moved to open the door. "The feeling is mutual," he said in a tone that traveled straight from her ears to her core. He raised her hand to his mouth and kissed the heel of it. It was an unlikely place, and it made her wonder what other unlikely places his mouth would feel just as good against.

"Goodnight, Sof," he said after she'd stepped out and shut the door, quietly so as not to draw too much attention. "If I had to get chased by an angry racist mob, I'm glad it was with you."

She let out a shocked laugh, and slammed her hand over her mouth.

She didn't watch him as he drove away. She saved that bit of laughter and warmth inside of her as she pulled herself back together. Back straight, shoulders dropped. She may have looked like a ragamuffin, but her poise would be impeccable when she walked into her home and faced her father.

chapter nine

Ivan knew he should have gone back to the store to pick up his father, but he had been so angry and confused that he hadn't wanted to share the small space of the car that still smelled of Sofie. Part of him was scared of how angry he was at his father. Not of losing his temper with his dad, but of losing his respect for him.

He'd driven home instead. As the steaming spray of the shower rinsed away the schmutz that'd been poured over him by those assholes at the diner, he remembered the way Sofie's eyes had gone round with fear when the bottle landed at her feet, and the way they had been liquid heat just before he kissed her in the alleyway. When he thought of his father, of the way he'd reacted to seeing him with Sofie, Ivan felt a deep shame descend upon him. It was the same shame that had haunted him since that day Sofie had protected and then lost her mother, as if his cowardice had brought down some wrath upon them all.

That kind of shame was an albatross. He'd borne its weight for so long—becoming bigger, stronger, and harder to injure had lightened his load but not removed it.

If he really thought about it, it was that shame that had driven him to the nonviolent resister meetings. He knew that he could stop a man with his sledgehammer fists and his hard left hook. But Jack had been wrong when he said throwing punches was Ivan's favorite thing; there was something redemptive about taking a punch that he couldn't explain, and to be able to do so for the greater good…

He was shadowboxing in his room when he heard the door open and his father return. His fists dropped to his sides as he heard his father's shuffling steps. Each one sounded like it only occurred through some extraordinary act of willpower, and through his anger Ivan reminded himself that he wasn't the only one who carried an invisible burden.

He walked down into the kitchen and saw his father standing in front of the sink, where water ran into an overflowing cup as he stared through the window. Mr. Friedman turned his head, as if he hadn't noticed his son walk into the room. "Ivan." He paused, his features hardening from soft and sad to defensive.

"What happened earlier today was a *shandeh un a charpeh*," Ivan said. The Yiddish wasn't usually the first thing his brain went to, but he didn't know the words in English that could convey his disappointment in his father.

"Yes," his father said. He put the glass down without drinking it. "It was shameful and disgraceful to be engaging in relations with that girl out in the open like a man with no sense of morality."

"Oh please, Pop," Ivan said. "If it had been Libby Weinberger out there with me, you wouldn't have been so quick to judge."

"First the boxing, now taking up with these rabble-rousers. You're not a schvartze—why don't you let these people fight their own battles? Do you think they would've helped us if the Nazis had made it to these shores?" Mr. Friedman rubbed at his brow. "When you were a boy you said that all you wanted to do was become a scholar, but then everything changed. Sometimes I wish we had never come to this place. Maybe it's being here that makes you such a disobedient son."

Ivan wished his father's words didn't have the ability to cut through him like a sharpened stone. He wanted to turn away from the anger and confusion he saw in his father's eyes, but he was a man now and would face this as a man would.

"You want a scholar? Chew on this: whether a person is gentile or Jew, they're entitled to *Kavod HaBriyot*—human dignity. Millions of people are being denied their dignity right now, and if I can do something to help change that, I will."

"What do you want? That I should be happy that you'll risk your life for the same people who come into my shop and call me a cheap Jew to my face?"

"Yes!" Ivan said. "People shouldn't have to be perfect to be seen as worthy of empathy."

His father stared at him, then shook his head. "I don't understand you. I don't understand anything anymore. I'm going to go talk to Rabbi Hirschman."

"Good. Make sure you ask him what he thinks of you being a bigot."

His father flinched and Ivan knew he had gone too far.
"Pop—"

The door slammed shut.

Ivan dragged himself up to his room, but he felt even more like a stranger in his own home than usual. He didn't know what had just happened between him and his father, but he felt like he'd just gone ten rounds only to be awarded a draw. He felt alone, and he knew there was only one way he wouldn't.

He picked up the phone beside his bed and dialed. When Sofie's voice came through, he smiled, in spite of everything.

"Hey. It's me. Did David and Henrietta get home okay?" he asked.

"Yes, they did. One of their friends was driving by and pulled them into the car." Her voice was stiff, and for a moment he thought she was angry with him. That thought hurt him far more than it should have, but when she remained on the line instead of hanging up, he realized she wasn't alone.

"Did things go okay with your father?" he asked.

"No." That was all she would give him. Her polite distance was making him miss her more than if he hadn't called.

He leaned back into his pillow. "I know this is probably crazy, given everything that happened today, but I can't stop thinking about that kiss. I think it was probably the best kiss I've ever had in my life."

There was a long pause, then he heard her breath shake on an exhale. That one little sound went through him like a static shock.

"Well, I don't have much experience in such matters, but...I feel the same way."

Those words eased past all of the ugliness of his encounter with his father, past the fear that had pumped through him when he thought Sofie might get hurt by the crowd.

"Sofie." He wasn't one for emotional displays, but it seemed that every minute that went by without him revealing how he felt was a moment lost. "I know you have lots more important stuff to worry about, but I'd like to take you out. I understand if you say no, but I can't stop thinking about you. I never have, if I'm being perfectly honest."

He thought about all the times over the years he'd seen someone who looked like her. A sudden hope would pound a ridiculous beat in his veins at the possibility...of what? It wouldn't be a second chance, really, but an opportunity to see what could happen.

He heard footsteps; the click of her heels on wood floor. Ivan held his breath, waiting for her to reject him. Their kiss had been amazing, but why would a woman like Sofie want anything to do with him?

"You know of someplace that we can go without starting a riot?" Her voice was quiet, like she was trying not to be overheard. Still, the playfulness in the tone of her serious question buoyed him.

"I have an idea," he said. "You free before church?"

"Sure."

"I'll pick you up at eight, then."

"Make it seven," she said. "Bye."

Ivan sat staring at the phone. Maybe he was crazy, but he was pretty sure she'd agreed to a date.

chapter ten

Sofie slipped through the doorway and out into the cool breeze of the Sunday morning dawn. She'd left a note for her father, and she prayed that the early hour she'd chosen meant that neither he nor her neighbors would see her slip into the Buick as it pulled in front of her house. She was dressed in her favorite outfit, a brown pencil skirt she'd spent hours sewing but never worn outside her room paired with an ivory shell. The little ruffles down the front of the shirt were both girlish and a hint at her feminine curves, so she offset it with a beige cardigan lest anyone else at church think her a hussy. After the way Ivan had made her feel, she was thinking maybe being a hussy wasn't such a bad thing.

"Hey," she said, nerves jangling as she settled into the seat and Ivan pulled away, taking them to some unknown destination. The smell of coffee and eggs wafted from the back of the car, making her stomach rumble.

"Hey," he said. The tight awkwardness of her greeting was contrasted by the smoothness of his deep voice. "I picked up breakfast for us. Milkshakes are apparently a great hair conditioner, but I decided I'd rather have food in me than on me today."

She laughed, even though it was a crazy thing to laugh about. They could have been killed the day before. Maybe she laughed because they hadn't been.

"Where are we going?" she asked. She wasn't afraid, at least not of Ivan.

"There's only one place I could think of where we could hang out without worrying too much," he said with a shrug. "It's only slightly better than the dumpsters from yesterday, so I understand if you don't want to stay."

He pulled up in front of a small brick building adorned with a sign that read "Jack's Brick House." A peeling painting of boxing gloves hung from the door, and junk that looked like castoffs from a mail-order fitness regimen littered the side of the building.

"I see what you mean by 'slightly,' but I'm guessing this is better than getting chased down Franklin Street."

She stepped out onto the cracked pavement, walking on tiptoe so her ivory pumps didn't get caught in any cracks. Ivan knelt and rummaged under a tire that was strewn in the grass, producing a key he then used to open the door.

"Are you supposed to be here?" Sofie asked. "I'm fine with breaking the law for a good cause, but a quiet breakfast isn't one of."

"Jack knows I come here when I need alone time." Ivan walked in, and she followed behind him. The enticing smell of breakfast was replaced by the smell of old sweat and leather, a combination that wasn't as bad as she'd imagined.

"Is this where you bring all the girls who are too dark to share a pop with at the five and dime?" Sofie asked as she sat in the folding chair Ivan directed her toward. She didn't mean for it to come out sounding like that—annoyed and accusatory—but she was risking a lot by trusting him enough to blindly follow him into the morning. If she was just another conquest, she deserved to know.

He dropped into the seat next to her and had the nerve to grin. "Would it make you jealous if I said yes?" he asked, handing her a warm paper cup of coffee. When she quirked a brow, he shook his head. "This gym is like my place of worship. I've been coming here since I was twelve, and I've probably spent more time here than anywhere else. If I bring a woman here, black or white, it's serious." He took a sip of coffee and pinned her with that intense gaze. "You're the first."

Sofie ignored the deeper meaning of his words and the way she wanted them to be true. But they couldn't be true, could they? "Ivan, there are a pair of crusty gym socks under my seat. This hardly rates as a first date, let alone a serious one."

For the first time since they'd reconnected, he pulled his gaze away from her in embarrassment. Regret stabbed at her that she'd been the one to make him feel foolish—she knew well enough what that felt like.

She fiddled with the edge of her coffee cup. "I didn't mean that. I'm glad to be here, crusty socks and all. Just…don't you think you're moving too fast?"

Ivan gave a short laugh and shook his head. "Let me give you a tour of the place." He was his usual playful and flirtatious self as he showed her around, even though Sofie could tell something was on his mind. He pointed out awards he and other boxers at the gym had won, showed her pictures of him sweaty and bloodied after victories. It was one thing to know Ivan was a fighter, but to see it…

He even moved differently in the gym, like a predator that struts through its own territory and knows no fear.

And he had reason for his pride. He walked her through his daily workout, and when he gave a brief demonstration of how to use the heavy bag, Sofie felt warmth that had nothing to do with the coffee she gulped rush through her body.

"Your…stamina is impressive," she said.

He grinned at her, and Sofie wondered just how it was possible for a man's mouth to be so enticing.

"I've been training since I was twelve, Sof. I'm the reigning champ for the region, so yeah, I've got good stamina." For a moment she wondered what had driven him to this violent sport, and then it clicked. Ivan had been weak, and now he was strong. That horrible moment from their past hadn't only affected her, it seemed. She wondered if he thought about that day as often as she did, but she refused to ruin the morning with that sadness.

"Reigning champ? You should really mention these things earlier when you're trying to get a girl to go steady with you," she teased.

He walked toward the ring and mounted the raised platform with ease. Once inside, he struck a Mr. Universe pose. "Well, I'm defending the title next weekend, if you want to see me fight."

The thought both thrilled and frightened her. What would it mean if she said yes? Would it mean she was his girl? How would people react if when he looked out into the crowd, it was her that he gazed at with affection? Sofie found she didn't care as much as she should have. For the moment, they were alone and Ivan was waiting for her, hand outstretched.

"Want to see what it's like from the inside?"

She'd thought she would be turned off by the smell and the boys' club atmosphere of the place, but she had to admit it was exciting, not least because she was alone with Ivan. She stepped out of her shoes and took his hand, giving a yip as he pulled her up and into the ring without even mussing her clothing.

"Wow," she said as she walked across the taut canvas. She bounced a bit, testing its give, and threw a few playful jabs his way. "You must feel like a king when you're in here with people cheering for you."

His eyes tracked her as she moved, like she was quarry that he didn't plan on letting escape.

"It has its perks," he said, walking toward her. She moved backward in response, following the moves of some pre-scripted dance between them. She didn't think Ivan walked toward his opponents like this as he backed them up against the ropes.

"Tell me something, Sofie." The tone of his voice made her breath catch. It was deeper, more sultry, and he knew exactly how to wield it. "Yesterday you told me that you were the one who convinced David and Henrietta to do that sit-in. You were the one who decided it was the right time to act. How long did it take you to come to that decision?"

Sofie felt like an animal that sees the snare tightening right before its capture. That feeling should have frightened her, but that wasn't why her heart was racing. "It just…happened. I just knew it was the right thing to do, and I trusted what I was feeling. For the first time in forever, I didn't second-guess myself or think of the proper thing to do."

Ivan moved closer. Her gaze was locked with his, but she felt the rope along her back vibrate as he grabbed it on either side of her.

"You're telling me that you rushed into a situation that could have gotten you kicked out of school, left you with a permanent record, or killed you, all based on a feeling?" His words were liquid insinuation. When she nodded, he tugged at the rope, bouncing her closer to him.

"I guess you could say rushing things isn't always such a bad idea then, huh?" He leaned down and kissed her, and again she felt the touch of his mouth in every part of her body. Her hands flattened over the hard muscles of his chest, and she felt his pecs jump as her palms made contact, like she was electrifying him.

His tongue eased a gentle entry, completely at odds with the coiled strength she felt in him, and she allowed it. When she opened for him, the gentleness faded. His tongue searched out hers with long, rough strokes. She knew his lips were soft, but they felt anything as they pressed against hers. One of his hands left the rope to cup her face as he kissed her into submission.

"Sofie." Her name was a plea. "I know we've just reconnected after all this time, and there's so much to do in the world. But I feel like...I really feel like we have something here."

"That's easy to say when your hand is in my shirt," she said with a breathless laugh. She glanced down to where his fingers had slid through the sleeve holes of her silky shell, stroking the sides of her breasts through her bra.

"That it is. Should I remove it?" he asked, stroking the back of his index finger over her taut nipple. Sofie arched her back, pushing into his touch. Her cheeks were aflame at the seediness of it all, but that didn't stop the pulsing between her legs or the way her drawers were soaked through. "That's not an answer," he said, and she felt the quick slide of his hand away from her.

"No," she gasped. "Don't." She knew there was nothing ladylike at all about the pure, blatant need that made her ache for his touch, but none of that mattered now.

He made a sound of approval.

"I need you to do something for me," he said. Sofie nodded, although she didn't think she would be capable of much. His big hands were cupping her breasts, his thumbs brushing over the tender peaks in a way that made her lose all consideration for what she should or shouldn't be doing. Each caress was tightening something in her, some degenerate part of her that craved Ivan in the middle of a boxing ring instead of a fine, upstanding citizen who wouldn't want to touch her until marriage.

"What is it?" she asked.

"Tell me that I'm moving too fast. Tell me that you don't feel something crazy between us." His voice was rough as he spoke.

"If I say that, will you stop touching me?" she asked. Her hands went to his waist, and her thumbs hooked into the belt loops on his jeans. She felt him tense, and his eyes closed for the briefest moment.

"This isn't an ultimatum, Sof. If you want me to make you come right here on the mat and then part ways forever, I'll do that." He gave a deep laugh at whatever expression flitted across her face. She wasn't completely untouched, but she was fairly certain no man had ever made her come, go, or anything in between before. He ran a hand over the buttons of her blouse and began sliding them out, one by one. "But I think there's more to us than wham bam thank you ma'am."

He lowered his forehead to hers. His hands slipped into her open shirt, his rough palms encircling the bare skin of her waist. "I've never stopped thinking of you, Sofronia. I always kept an eye out for you, hoping one day we'd see each other. Then I'd either know I was wrong and move on, or this would happen."

Sofie ran her hands up his chest, over the corded muscles at his neck, and threaded her fingers at his nape. "What do you mean by *this*?"

"That I'd see you and want to be with you more than ever." His eyes were closed, like he was confessing something painful. She ran her fingertips over his long lashes, and then over the bumps at the bridge of his nose.

"Ivan...what we're doing right now? It feels right. That's what my instinct is telling me. Maybe the crazy is catching, but I want to be with you too." His eyes fluttered open and she was flummoxed by the naked need she saw in his gaze. No one had ever looked at her like that before. She swallowed and then said the first thing that came into her mind. "I want you to touch me the way you look at me, like me being nice is the last thing you're thinking of."

His head tilted quick as a flash and then his mouth was on hers. He kissed her without mercy, as if her request had allowed him to unleash the true level of his desire for her. He wasn't rough, despite his vocation, but he kissed her as if it was the last thing he would do in this world and he wanted to make sure it was done well. It was all Sofie could do to remain standing; not because her knees were weak, but because if she pulled him to the ground like she wanted to, her church clothes would be ruined and there'd be even more gossip swirling around. Ivan backed her up against a corner post and gently untucked her shirt. His hands groped at her hips and her backside, and then he threw his head back in frustration.

"Where's the zipper?" he asked.

Sofie froze. What was she doing there with him? Was she ready for whatever he had in mind? And then he smiled at her, that sheepish, chip-toothed smile, and she reached for the hidden zipper at the side of the skirt without hesitation. "I might be too good of a seamstress," she said as she worked it down.

"I've noticed," Ivan said. "Even your most demure outfit has the opposite effect on me." Then he slid his hand into the loosened waist of her skirt and rubbed her through her panties, and all thoughts of sewing techniques went out of Sofie's head. One of his hands went behind her waist to lift and support her, while his mouth forged a trail from the sensitive skin of her neck down to her thin bra. He licked through the lacy fabric she had worn with him in mind, as if some delinquent part of her had hoped he'd see it. Well, he was seeing it now, and tasting it too. He lapped at her sensitive tips, swirling his tongue around and grabbing her nipple between his teeth, even as his fingers groped their way into her drawers and massaged her sensitive nub.

"Oh," she breathed quietly. She felt more than that little sound, but her training was kicking in, even when she should be wild and free. She even had to sin like a lady.

Ivan glanced up at her and shook his head with a glint in his eye that didn't bode well for her.

"None of that dormouse stuff, Sofronia." His voice was rough and his hand picked up the pace to match. Callused fingertips pressed harder against that slit of pleasure, and a remarkable feeling flowed through Sofie, like all of the pain and sadness and happiness that she had bottled up over the years was suddenly pushing to get out all at once.

"Ivan!" Her voice was louder than she'd spoken in years, and when he sucked at her neck and curled a finger inside of her, she broke and let out a cry that even the lead in the choir couldn't have matched. Pleasure pulsed and pulsed through her body, divine and unrepentant. Her voice echoed around the gym as she sagged back against the post and simply let herself feel for once.

"Good to know those pipes are still working." He kissed the hollow of her neck as he rebuttoned her blouse, and a different kind of thrill went through her, one she had never experienced. Not during that fumbling childhood kiss with David or on the double dates she went on with Henrietta. She felt like part of a duo, two people who could change things…together.

They'd just climbed down from the ring when the front door swung open and an older black man with the body of someone half his age walked in.

His eyes widened at the sight of Sofie, and the powerful togetherness she felt started to fade as every horrible thing the man could be thinking ran through her mind. Then he smiled. "Is this the lady who's had you distracted during your sparring matches all week?"

Sofie looked at Ivan and was shocked to see he was blushing. Blushing, after all that talk in the ring. "Jack, Sofie. Sofie, Jack," he said.

"Nice to meet you, young lady. And I know that pretty face is familiar for a reason."

He handed her the morning paper. There she was, sitting primly at the Special K counter, surrounded by a mob of angry men. It seemed that her years of training had one benefit: she looked like a perfect lady, her rigidness making the men around her look even more like barbarians. David and Henrietta appeared to be studying in the midst of the melee, but Ivan was regarding her with an adoring grin. She'd seen men look at women like that before, but that Ivan was regarding her in such a way for everyone to see...

"Oh dear Lord," she said. She could already hear her father going on about how she'd humiliated him, how his job was in jeopardy, and the other things he'd listed as he'd guilted her the night before. But something else caught her eye. NASH LEADS NASHVILLE RIDERS, a headline beside the picture screamed. Sofie clutched the paper, reading excitedly.

"The rides aren't over," she said, looking at Ivan. "Students are leaving from Nashville and encouraging others to ride to Mississippi. They believe that if the rides stop because of the incidents in Anniston and Birmingham, the blow to the movement will be hard to recover from." Sofie again felt the sense of unity that was a newfound thing for her—she wasn't the only one who felt that way. These young people in Nashville and others around the country were going to get on buses and head to

Mississippi, and she was going to join them. She felt that sense of purpose flow through her again.

"Now, a lunch counter is one thing, but getting on that bus is another," Jack said. He looked at Ivan as if he had some say in the matter, but Ivan raised his hands.

"If she wants to go, we'll go. It'll probably take a few days to get everything together and scrape together money for tickets. Besides, you have your finals and I have my match. We can leave Saturday morning."

Sofie had never felt such a quick rise and drop in spirits. "A whole week? Do you know what can happen in a week? We have to go now while the world is still watching. A week from now the Soviets might launch a nuke and no one will care about whether some kids are causing a scene in the Deep South."

"If you miss your exams, won't you flunk out for the semester?" Ivan asked. "Think about what you're saying."

Sofie felt her instinct to buckle to authority kick in. Ivan was right. She stood to lose so much if she skipped out, and not just her—her father's savings and his hope for the first generation to go to school would also be lost. But she couldn't sit in a classroom while her fellow students were making sacrifices of their own.

"There will be other semesters, Ivan. There may not be other Freedom Rides. I'm going to go, whether you decide to or not."

"You can't go by yourself," he said. He snatched the paper from her, eyes scanning the cramped newsprint. "These students have signed their last wills and testaments. They're ready to die. Are you?"

When their eyes met in challenge, Sofie felt something in her heart give way like a crumbling ledge. He didn't believe in her. She still felt his touch on her body. He'd made her feel wonderful but more wonderful still had been the thought that finally someone had thought her capable of more than being a goody two shoes. She'd been mistaken on that account.

"If that's what it takes," she said, squaring her shoulders. "I don't see how you being there will change anything. If you want to stay, stay, but don't you dare presume to know what I'm willing to give up for the movement."

"Oh no, girl," Jack said, moving to stand between them. "Don't you try to lay a guilt trip on the boy because he has priorities. He's been working toward this fight for years. Almost half his life!" The man looked so disappointed in her, as if she was trying to steal Ivan's glory, that she couldn't help but think of her father.

"This isn't an ultimatum," she said weakly. Jack leaned in to hear her because her voice had barely carried to him. Had that loud, resounding cry earlier really come from her?

"I should get you to church," Ivan said. He took her arm, but his touch was like that of a stranger. She should have been angry, but the fire in her chest went cold. Disappointment replaced it, spreading through her body so that she felt sluggish as she walked out after him. She'd allowed herself to think that Ivan was different, but he was just one more person to let down, and Sofie didn't think she needed that in her life. She was full up on people who would gladly judge her.

The ride to her church was silent. As loss crept up on her, she tried to remind herself that a week ago she hadn't been thinking of Ivan at all. If after today she never saw him again, the last seven days would have been an aberration and he would recede to the vaults of her memory once again. She didn't believe that for a second, but if it got her through the rest of the day, she'd try to.

"I wish I could leave sooner than Saturday," he said as he dropped her off three blocks from her church, as she'd requested. "But I've worked so hard for this. There are going to be promoters there, and this could be my chance at the big time, and a chance to help Jack get his name on the map. I'd be letting everyone at the gym down if I didn't fight."

Sofie tried to muster a smile, but couldn't quite pull it off. "I understand. You're going after what you believe in. I didn't believe in anything for a long time but keeping my head down and not being noticed. But now I feel like I can do something, be part of something." She took a deep breath. "I won't wait for you."

"Why? I don't get the rush." His eyes widened as if she had just dumped ice over him.

"Because even a docile girl like me has to stand up for herself sometime, and that time is right now." She leaned in and kissed him then, despite her disappointment. If things were to go awry and the worst should occur, she didn't want to regret not having one last touch of his soft lips. Even if things didn't go wrong, she couldn't expect some pledge of faithfulness after just a few days. She was sure some woman or other would be hanging around the ring to either celebrate or console him on Friday night. "Goodbye, Ivan."

"I'll call you later!" he called after her as she walked down the street. She hated the desperation in his voice, but she didn't look back. She was already listing the next steps of her plan.

chapter eleven

S ofie had flinched when she walked through the doors of the church, but she hadn't combusted, despite her interlude with Ivan. If the Lord didn't see fit to punish her, she could withstand whatever anyone else had to say.

"I saw you in the paper this morning," Mrs. Pierce said when Sofie greeted her in passing. She regarded Sofie shrewdly, but then the church pianist grabbed her to discuss the same thing, and Sofie breathed a sigh of relief. The last thing she needed was the woman harping on her yet again.

After fidgeting her way through service beside her stiff and silent father, Sofie found she was actually looking forward to the after-church meetup. Everyone seemed to be buzzing about the Freedom Rides and what it meant for the movement. She heard a few dissenters, but she hoped that they were a minority. Although she didn't need the support of the majority for what she had planned.

After Melba announced that the quilting circle had been moved from Tuesday to Wednesday, Sofie stood and cleared her throat. As usual, everyone ignored her, but then she remembered her voice echoing around the gym that morning and used it.

"I'd like to make a request," she said loudly. Everyone stopped what they were doing and looked at her in surprise. "Many of you are talking about the Freedom

Rides today. I would like to join the movement and head down to Mississippi, but I'm afraid I don't have the funds for a Greyhound ticket. If there are any of you who see the same righteousness in this cause that I do, I would appreciate a donation. I may not be Martin or Malcolm, but I'd like to do my part to help put an end to the fear we live with every day, that one misstep can result in our injury or death just because of the color of our skin. I think these rides can help do that. Thank you."

She dropped down into her seat. She didn't know what to expect now; that was the drawback of behaving impulsively.

Sofie noticed Mrs. Pierce stand across the room. "If I may?" The words were polite, but the question was hypothetical. Everyone turned toward the woman's perfectly modulated voice.

"Now, I'm sure many of you have seen today's paper. If you haven't, you should know that our own Sofie Wallis was on the front page, seen staging a sit-in." Sofie's face went hot and her mouth went dry. She waited along with the rest of the congregation to see what Mrs. Pierce would say. Her fellow churchgoers were suspiciously quiet.

"The movement for our people's freedom has been a topic of conversation every Sunday since I was a child. I've contributed my time and my money and my tears, and I have no regrets about that. But when I saw Sofie on that front page, looking the spitting image of her mama, I couldn't help but think, 'This child is brave! Braver than I've ever been.'" Mrs. Pierce's eyes were glossy and her usually steady voice had taken on a bit of a tremor. "We all remember Delia and how she always spoke her mind. I think...I think she would be very proud of you, girl. I'm proud of you. I'll cover the cost of the ticket, on one condition."

"What's that, Sister Pierce?" someone shouted out, saving Sofie the trouble.

Mrs. Pierce smiled. "After hearing the strength in the request she just made, straight from the diaphragm, I never want to hear her whisper-singing in my choir again."

Sofie couldn't stop the happy tears that spilled from her eyes then. She remembered the day her mother had come running from the Freidmans' kitchen, and how in the brief moment before she began to break up the fight, before she died, Mama had seen Sofie holding her own against the group of boys. All she'd wanted was to do her mother proud, and hearing those words from such an unexpected source was all the more shocking.

"I'll buy the ticket." A hand clamped on her shoulder, and Sofie held it with both of hers.

"Daddy?" She looked up to see her father with tears in his eyes that matched her own.

"I just wanted to keep you safe. You're all I have left." He sighed. "Delia always said that if I held you too close I could squeeze the life out of you, and that's what I did, isn't it?"

His shoulders heaved, and Sofie jumped and hugged him close. "You did what you thought was best," she said. That didn't take away the years of hurt, but one thing the movement was teaching her was that to move forward there had to be reconciliation. She didn't know if she forgave her father yet, but she loved him regardless.

"When are you heading out?" he asked in a hoarse voice.

"There's a bus leaving tonight."

"Then let's go pack your bags. I'll take you to dinner and you can tell me all about this movement. I still think it's crazy, but if it's important to you..." He hugged her even tighter. Sofie couldn't have asked for a better gift.

chapter twelve

I t was only when Sofie had boarded the bus that night, tucking her small travel bag under her uncomfortable seat that she realized she'd never taken a trip by herself. She'd been so caught up in the end result that she hadn't paid attention to the fine details, like how frightening it would be to do this alone. The phone had started ringing as she and her father left the house, and Sofie knew without picking up that it was Ivan. She'd let it ring. She remembered the way he'd sounded when they spoke on the phone—quiet, intimate—and felt the foolish urge to cry. She didn't know how or why she had let him get to her, especially when others had been trying to line her up as a ready-made wife since she'd turned eighteen.

She craved Ivan's presence, but she told herself that she could never miss anyone more than her mother, and she'd lived through that. Barely. Getting over Ivan would be easy in comparison, even if the pain in her chest indicated otherwise.

Sofie slept more deeply than was probably wise on public transportation, and woke to the sun shining across fields of Carolina tobacco. Her throat tightened at the beauty of the sight, and at the fading dream of her mother sitting beside her through the night as the bus rolled over state lines.

The trip was uneventful, and as other young people with the same intention boarded at various stops, she learned that the police had changed their tactics; allowing mobs to beat the riders was no longer an option thanks to the news media. The trip was relatively safe now, according to them, and there was no need to guess what was waiting ahead of them. "They're sending everyone to the farm. Parchman Farm," a theology student from Georgia said when he'd settled into the seat across from her. "Still illegal, but they struck up some deal with Bobby Kennedy to make sure we don't get our heads caved in. It only took one of his men ending up in the hospital before they cared enough to do that."

Sofie had heard enough blues songs to know that Parchman was the most reviled prison in the country, but when they finally pulled into the Greyhound station in Jackson singing "We Shall Overcome," she felt no fear. She marched out with the other riders and headed straight for the Whites Only waiting room.

"We are not afraid, we are not afraid, we are not afraid, toda-aa-ay!" She pushed the words out into the cloudless spring sky, her voice dwarfing all the others, even as the police officers stepped in front of them. Through the dirt-specked glass, Sofie could see men milling about in the waiting room, the same ugly look on their faces that she'd seen in the Special K diner.

The officers wore riot helmets, and their blue uniform shirts had stains where they'd been sweat through and then dried again. Sofie kept singing, and her voice didn't falter, but a little seed of fear sprouted in her when one of the officers pulled out his billy club and took a step forward. His eyes locked on Sofie—perhaps drawn by her voice—and he was on her in two steps.

He grabbed her roughly by the collar of the jacket she wore over her simple dress. She heard the stitching she had worked so hard on rip and then she was flying this way and that. "You think you can just come marching in here singing a happy little tune and change things?" The visor of his helmet was up and his sweaty pink face was much too close to hers. He pushed her back and then gave her an extra shove with the edge of his baton, sending her against the glass door of the waiting room. "We treat our niggers good here. You ain't doing nothing but causing trouble."

Sofie didn't have time to process the madness of the man's words. The door began to shake behind her. She could hear the taunts and leers of the men who had been waiting to greet the riders with violence, but she didn't hear the singing of her friends any longer. A shove from the door pushed her to her knees, and the burning scrape of jagged concrete surprised her into the truth. The other students had been wrong; these men were going to hurt her, Bobby Kennedy be damned.

Sofie looked up at the officer, at the hatred in his eyes that she would never comprehend. "I'm not your nigger or anyone else's," she said. "And if you think I'm causing trouble now, I'll have you know I'm just getting started."

The officer lifted his baton, but Sofie didn't look away. Her heart was pounding so hard that she could barely hear the men egging the officer on.

"Bill, what the hell are you doing? Get that girl in the goddamned wagon before a reporter shows up!" The officer lowered his baton at the command and grabbed Sofie roughly by the arm.

"Have fun at Parchman, Sweetie," he growled as he pushed her into the wagon. "Ain't no cameras there to keep you safe."

"Sofie!" Michael pulled her inside, and she felt like a lost lamb returning to the fold. "You're shaking. We turned around and you were gone. What happened?"

A woman next to her held her hand for a moment, and Sofie took a deep breath.

"I'm fine."

The wagon was hot, and they sat baking for what seemed like an eternity compared to the long bus ride. They sang We Shall Overcome again, and that song changed to a church hymn, and then the national anthem, and then someone quickly taught them a call-and-respond song made especially for the protests. The singing fortified something in Sofie and her newfound compatriots. Their voices together became something more than just sound, but a physical force beating back the negativity around them. Sofie stank, and she needed a shower and coffee and for her First Amendment rights to be respected, but she closed her eyes and sang like it was the only thing that mattered.

"Can we take 'em over, Bill?" Sofie heard one of the officers ask.

"Get these assholes out of here," the officer who had attacked her replied. "I'm gonna have that shit music stuck in my head all night."

The door to the wagon closed and Sofie felt an inkling of real panic wiggling her belly. That officer had been right—they would have no protections at Parchman. It was where they sent people to rot. What if she never got out? What if this had all been a terrible mistake?

Her breath came in a shallow, ragged gasp, and she wanted to push the door to allow fresh air to enter. The realization that she couldn't sent her further into a panic. She jumped to her feet.

"It's okay, sister," Michael, the theological student, said. "We're here with you. God is here with us and cloaking us in His mercy. But it would also help if you sat down and took a deep breath."

Sofie tried to fight the animal instinct to kick and claw at the door, but then, as if God had, indeed, had mercy on her, it swung open. Sofie's panic fled, chased away by pure shock that gave her gooseflesh even in the sweltering wagon.

"Ivan!"

He stood there looking quite unconcerned with the police officer who was pulling him by the collar of his suit. That he was dressed so finely, in a crisp three-piece suit complete with a vest, was almost as surprising as his presence.

"Were you avoiding my calls? I tried to tell you I was coming. I *just* missed that Greyhound last night," he said. "Probably better that I had to take the Trailways, though. Staying true to the cause might have been a little difficult sitting next to you on a dark bus."

"Oh dear Lord," Sofie said, covering her eyes with her hands and dropping back into her seat. She peeped through her fingers to see Ivan crawl inside and sit on the floor at her feet, and then the door slammed shut.

"Hello, everyone," he said, grinning that grin of his, and the apprehension in the bus melted away.

"Welcome to the Parchman express," Michael said, reaching over to clap him on the shoulder. "You ready for the chain gang, brother?"

"Breaking rocks is a great way for a boxer to stay in shape," Ivan said. "I'll look at it as a state-funded bodybuilding club."

Sofie stared at him as they bumped along, not quite knowing what to say.

"What happened to your knee?" he asked, pulling a handkerchief from his pocket and pressing at the bleeding abrasion.

"Officer Bill," she replied.

His expression clouded at that. "Definitely good that I was on the Trailways then."

Sofie wanted to reach out and touch him, but she was worried he would vanish if she did. He couldn't really be there with her, could he?

"What about your match? I hope you didn't come out of guilt." She'd never been happier to see someone, but she didn't want to be the impetus for his decision. A thought struck her, and she crossed her arms over her chest. "Or because you thought I couldn't do this by myself."

Ivan sighed and draped his hands over his legs. "I came because you were right. I wanted to help, and waiting until after I'd knocked some guy's lights out wasn't the way to do it. So I called Calvin and told him why I had to forfeit. Of course, he didn't want to win like that, so we agreed to reschedule. We talked for a long time, actually—I wouldn't be surprised if he was making the ride too."

He took a deep breath. "And because I knew I would miss you too much," he said in a low voice. He took her hand and kissed the back of it, a chaste motion, like something she read in her Arthurian legends. Now she knew why Guinevere had fallen.

He was looking at her with that intense gaze, the one that made Sofie feel both vulnerable and protected at once. She didn't look away even as the wagon bumped along on the rutted country road. She'd made the journey down by herself, and she knew she could do it alone. But Ivan sitting beside her felt as right as the decision to come itself.

"Well, if I have to be thrown in the worst prison in the US, I'm glad it's with you," she said. The bus stopped and idled at the gates. Sofie knew that she and the other riders had a hard few weeks ahead of them, but her hand was in Ivan's, and together they could do anything.

chapter thirteen

Three weeks later

Sofie was too thin. Ivan ran his hand over her ribcage and the dip of her belly as she slept deeply beside him in the lumpy motel bed. They'd have to leave soon to continue the second leg of their journey home from Mississippi, but she needed her rest after the ordeal they'd been through. Being placed in separate cells with the other Freedom Riders had given them some level of safety, but many of the guards had tried to break them. Food had been scant and, when it arrived, nearly inedible. Mattresses and toothbrushes and privacy had been taken away as punishment for the songs they sang constantly to keep themselves motivated. As more and more young people from across the country joined the ride, the cells were filled to many times over their capacities, which was the only reason Ivan and Sofie had been released.

They'd been able to send each other notes through prison workers sympathetic to the Freedom Riders' plight, but he'd still missed her something terrible. Their reunion on the wagon, after he thought he'd lost her for good, had been too short. Having her warm and smooth beside him as he'd imagined for so long—it was more powerful than any rush of endorphins after a boxing match.

He loved her, even if it was too early to tell her that. She'd already skittered away when he'd jokingly dropped to one knee when they met outside the gates of Parchman, reminding him marriage was illegal where they were from, so he tucked that idea away for a time when she was ready, if she ever was. Ivan wasn't in any rush, despite the fact that he'd nearly spilled before he touched her the night before.

His member stiffened at the thought of their first time making love. They'd both known what awaited them as they wandered from the bus depot; even the disapproving look the man at the motel's front desk gave them had done nothing to dampen how much they wanted each other.

Nothing could stop that, it seemed.

The room they were in wasn't anywhere near good enough for Sofie, but it beat the amenities at Parchman. After weeks of crawling in his skin, the shower at the motel had seemed like a spa. When Sofie had emerged from the bathroom and laid her towel down on the bed, fear and determination and lust in her gaze, it'd seemed like whatever Christians must imagine heaven to be like.

Sofie stirred beneath his hand and turned sleepy brown eyes on him, disturbing his recollection of the way she'd been so pliant beneath him just hours before. Ivan felt pinned by her gaze, like he'd been hit by a surprise blow.

"Did you know you laugh in your sleep?" he asked because he couldn't think of anything else to say. "It's kind of creepy. What were you dreaming about?"

Her eyes shimmered with mirth as she shook her head. "I don't remember. All I know is you were there, and that made everything all right."

Warmth rushed through Ivan, converging at a particular point in his chest

"Something's poking me," she said suddenly. Her voice was husky with sleep, but she was alert enough to reach down and embrace the hardening length of him in her fist. Pleasure marched up Ivan's spine as she smiled at him innocently while caressing him beneath the sheets. "There's a strange object in the bed with us. Maybe I should investigate."

"Ever intrepid Sofronia," he said, the S in her name coming out as a hiss because her touch felt so good.

He closed his fist around her hand as she stroked him, preventing her from making him blow too fast. When she released him, uncertain, he rolled over so that she was beneath him. He slid his arms beneath her back so that he cradled her, and settled between her legs, teasingly close to her warm entrance. "My, my, my. Little miss church girl sure has developed an appetite."

Sofie ran her hands over his back and up through his hair. "I'll have you know the most erotic thing I've ever read was at church. Song of Solomon," she said. The word *erotic* on her lips was enough to make his hips shift forward, seeking the pleasure of her warmth, but then she kept going. "First line: 'Let him kiss me with the kisses of his mouth.'"

She stared at him expectantly, and he did as she commanded. His lips grazed hers, but she kissed him deeply, using her hands to pull his mouth down onto hers. He groaned into that kiss, and she licked at his lips, sliding her tongue in and taking what she wanted. That Sofie felt no need to be timid with him sent a shiver of pleasure through his body, one he felt in his toes.

He pulled his head back for a moment and caught her eye. "That's Old Testament, baby. Ketuvim. If you think I wasn't flipping to that section and having impure thoughts at the back of the synagogue, then you don't know me very well." She pressed her head back into the pillow and laughed, and Ivan had never seen anything more beautiful. He kissed her chin. "I have my own favorite line from the Songs."

Sofie put a hand over his mouth. "Wait! Let me guess." She stared at him and then graced him with a wicked smile. "'Let my beloved come to his garden, and eat its choicest fruits.'"

Ivan licked at her palm, and she shivered as she pulled it away. "I guess you do know me," he said.

"Not as well as I'd like to." She reached between them and guided him inside of her. They both gasped, and Ivan took another harsh breath as her tightness squeezed along the length of his shaft. He bit his lip, hoping that the pain would distract from the pleasure that was threatening to send him over the edge much too soon.

"Oh!" He looked down into her face and was met with a look of surprised satisfaction.

"This feels better than last night, I imagine?" he asked as he thrust into her. He was glad his voice didn't come out a strained squeak—just because he felt like a teenager with no control didn't mean he had to sound like one.

She pressed her nails into his back and arched beneath him. "Yes, Ivan. Yes."

"Good," he growled. "Let's get reacquainted, then."

After that, there was no banter, no chitchat, just the overwhelmingly sweet pleasure of teaching a good girl some very naughty things.

I van watched Sofie step out of Jack's Brick House and hand a cookie to a little girl with round cheeks and two puffy pigtails, and something in him shifted yet again.

They'd returned home two days before, and had each been busy catching up with the life they'd left behind for a Mississippi jail. Now they were at Jack's, not for training, but to celebrate history—a history he was now a part of. People were as convivial as they had been in prison, but instead of being crammed into a cell as they laughed and sang to pass the time, they were outside surrounded by blue sky, green grass, and the smell of meat on the grill. It was a shock to the system to go from mealy bread to tender sides of beef and juicy burgers. Ivan could barely eat, but he was happy to sit and observe.

He felt an overwhelming tenderness as Sofie interacted with Jack and his wife, the people who had been a secondary family to him. They weren't so different, despite the way people on the street stared as they walked hand in hand. And they'd be all right, in the long run. Their road wouldn't be easy, but they weren't the first to travel it. Besides, easy was for chumps.

Jack stood up from where he was talking to some of the younger boxers, the only people who hadn't heard the story of how he beat Rocky Marciano in an exhausting sparring match but would never be credited. As the boys chatted excitedly after the climax of the tale, Jack dug around in an icebox for a soda and then chimed one of the ringside bells he'd brought outside for the occasion.

"Everyone, I just want to thank you for coming to this first annual Juneteenth Celebration at Jack's Brick House. I don't know why it took me so long to honor my grandfather in this way, but this year seems like a good year to start." He paused and took a sip of soda, and his mouth pulled into a grimace. Anyone who knew Jack understood that meant he was fighting deep emotion. Better to look mean than to look weak, he always said. "Sometimes it seems like the battle for freedom for our people is never-ending. It can make you bitter, when you think about the unfairness of it all. But right now, we're seeing a new generation taking up the mantle. I wish these youngins didn't have to, but I can't help but celebrate their determination, their focus, and their bravery."

He glanced at Sofie, who had walked over to stand beside Ivan.

"On this Juneteenth, I want to remember our people's liberation from slavery, but also to remind everyone of the continuing journey. I might not live to see it happen, but one day we will truly be free."

He scowled and took a sip of his soda as the guests began to clap. Ivan felt a lump in his throat as he watched Jack's puff-tailed granddaughter skip up to console her Pop-Pop. If he and Sofie had a child, would he experience the same gut-wrenching fear that Jack must feel for all the young ones in his family?

"Sofie, the boy next to you says you can sing. Can you hum a little something for us?" Jack asked, trying to draw the attention away from himself. Ivan felt Sofie tense. He'd heard her voice across the yard at Parchman every now and again, but this was different. That night in the motel she'd told him how she hadn't sung since Miss

Delia's death, and she still hadn't here in their hometown. But she looked up at him and asked, "Will you be my backup singer?"

He smiled at her and saw how her eyes brightened with emotion when he did. "Only if you'll be my ring-girl at the fight next month."

She rolled her eyes. "Oh please. I still have some sense of propriety, Ivan. Just not in the bedroom. Now follow my lead."

She turned to face the crowd and took a deep breath, and when she opened her mouth and belted out the first line, everyone else's mouths dropped open too. The dormouse had gone into hibernation, and Sofie let her voice unfurl full-bellied and proud, as if she wanted Miss Delia to hear, wherever she was.

"This little light of mine, I'm gonna let it shine." She glanced at him with a smile that made him want to kiss her, but she'd stomp his toes if he tried it. "This little light of mine, I'm gonna let it shine."

Ivan joined her on the next line, knowing no one would be paying attention to his voice anyway. It didn't matter.

This was Sofronia, and he'd follow her anywhere.

epilogue

1964, Virginia

Sofie placed the to-do list on the freshly scrubbed laminate of the kitchen counter. Like everything else in the small room, it was a bright, buttery yellow; something straight from the 1955 edition of *House Beautiful* magazine. She'd hated it when she and Ivan first moved in, but it was actually nice to come home to something cheery when the neighbors all gave you the cold shoulder. She wondered if it was the afro she was growing out; when she'd viewed the apartment, her hair had been straightened with a hot comb—so that it was limp and lifeless, nonthreatening. People had only been mildly rude then, not openly hostile. Ivan joked that it was because he refused to do their taxes. They both knew the real reason.

She scanned the list, or rather the complex groupings of items, complete with headings, sublists, and footnotes. The orderly rows of fastidious handwriting made her feel in control, even when she was so nervous that she was sure she'd sweat through the pretty pink A-line dress she'd sewn specially for today. Under the heading HANNUKKAH, she'd written little notes that she could reference if she got too nervous: *Maccabee story; oil is important; mitzvah (find out from Ivan); berakot (blessings) – l'hadlik, she-asah nisim, shehekianu; do not blow out the shamash; ask Mr. Friedman to touch his horns.*

"Ivan!" she shouted in amused annoyance. He liked to make his own additions to her lists, especially when he knew her nerves were frayed.

He stepped out of their bedroom, still in the process of pulling his simple white t-shirt down over his muscular chest and abdomen. She caught a glimpse of smooth skin and a dark trail of hair, and then he tucked the shirt into his Levi's. His dark eyes homed in on her as he walked toward the kitchen. Maybe it was his bruised cheek, a remnant of his last match, that gave his approach a thrilling hint of danger. Or the way his full lips pulled up into the kind of smile that usually ended with her bent over the arm of the couch, the kitchen sink, or the dining room table. Everywhere but the bed, which good girls like her had been taught was the *only* place for such activities. She knew better now.

Now, Ivan walked up and gripped the counter on either side of her, hemming her in. The old Sofie would have been embarrassed at the way he made her blush like a sinner at a church revival. The new Sofie was still embarrassed, but leaned her hips forward, loving the contact with his muscular thighs.

"I've told you not to tamper with my lists," she said, holding his gaze. His hands still gripped the counter, but now they slid along the metal trim, both of them reaching her hips simultaneously. His hands briefly cupped her curves as they moved upward, and then encircled her waist. The weight of them resting there was just as potent as a caress, maybe more so; it was a silent reminder of everything he could do to her.

Ivan grinned, heedless of the chipped front tooth that he was usually embarrassed to reveal; she found it so endearing her heart hurt. "And I've told you that if you intend to make me sit through a Hanukkah dinner with both of our fathers, I'm going to need something to look forward to besides malevolent stares from one side of the table and blatant disapproval from the other. I get enough of those as it is."

His hands began to make small smoothing motions over her hips, as if he were fixing her dress or contemplating taking it off. She never knew with him.

He lifted one shoulder. "I figure you can ask my dad if he has horns under his yarmulke, I can ask your dad if he wants some watermelon, and they'll both be so mad about those put-downs they'll forget we're living in sin. It'll be a gas."

She made an incredulous noise and pushed at his solid shoulder, which didn't budge. "If you even breathe the word 'watermelon' in front of my father, he'll stick that menorah where the sun don't shine so fast it'll still be lit. And I'll help him."

"Weren't you the one who talked me into the whole nonviolence thing?" he asked, brows raised.

"Violence is never the answer," Sofie replied solemnly. "Unless you sass my daddy. Then I'll have to put a hurtin' on you."

He laughed. "Okay, then. I guess I'll use my endurance training to withstand the family fun we'll have to sit through tonight." His smile faded as he ducked his head and looked into her eyes. He ran one callused knuckle over her jaw line. "Sof? What's wrong?"

"I'm…I'm nervous." She knew Ivan was too, which accounted for his joking, but this was important to her. She wanted Ivan's father to like her. She wanted her father to accept Ivan. She wanted to have the fun family gatherings she remembered from her childhood, before her mother passed away, not an acrimonious night where everyone merely tolerated one another. Was that not in the cards for her, just because she'd fallen in love with a Jewish brawler instead of an Alpha Phi Alpha?

Ivan looked down at her, that crushing tenderness that was so at odds with everything else about him etched onto his face. "Listen to me. I've watched you stare down an officer with a rifle pointed in your face. I've seen…" He paused, closed his eyes briefly. His Adam's apple bobbed. "I've seen you take a punch from a full-grown man that might have knocked me on my ass. You didn't cry, and you never flinched. You're the bravest woman I know. One holiday dinner with our fathers? Piece of cake, baby."

Sofie's eyes heated with tears. They'd been through so much in the last three years. But they'd been through it all together, which had made it tolerable. "You're going to mess up my makeup, you schmoe."

"See? You've got the Yiddish down already. Dad'll welcome you to the tribe with open arms." She leaned her forehead against his chest as she laughed. He smelled like Ivory soap and starch, even if he didn't act like a man who would. "As for your makeup; yeah, you're gonna have to reapply it."

"What?" When she looked up, his mouth was already on a collision course with hers. Their lips met and the same sweet explosion rocked her, the one that lit her up every time. She'd thought kissing the same man would get boring after months and years, but the press of Ivan's pouty lips and the slide of his tongue just did it for her. His fingers inched her dress up her thighs.

"This'll help with the nerves," he said as he pressed her into the counter and began kissing his way down her neck.

His mouth trailing kisses toward her breasts was far from calming, but she tugged his t-shirt out of his jeans and ran her hands over the warm swath of skin he had flashed earlier. "I'm willing to give anything a try," she said.

Hours later, Sofie retreated to the kitchen in defeat. She opened the door of the Big Chill fridge and contemplated crawling inside.

Mr. Friedman was distant and overly formal, to the point that he seemed almost angry at her. When she explained that she'd had the menorah shipped from New York City by a friend she'd met during the protests, he hadn't reacted with delight, or even been impressed. Instead, he'd critiqued her placement of the candelabrum, saying it wasn't public enough, and had responded with a huff when she placed it in the front window, despite the risk to her curtains. When night fell, Ivan lit the shamash and invited his father to light the candle representing the first night of Hanukkah and to sing the shehekianu. Mr. Friedman had put him off. The shamash still burned alone, a flickering reminder that nothing she could do would please the man.

Her father was just as bad. There were good days and bad days with him, and this wasn't one of the good. He pretended not to comprehend the Jewish customs, as if taking the body of Christ at communion made much more sense. Every attempt at secular conversation Ivan threw out was rebuffed, or somehow came back around to how her mother was rolling in her grave knowing her Sofie was living in sin. He played deaf when Sofie reminded him that the law wouldn't allow them to marry, that miscegenation—the ugliness of the word made her shudder—wasn't legal in Virginia.

The two older men didn't speak to each other at all, as if Sofie's mother hadn't worked for Mr. Friedman all those years ago. As if there weren't so many important threads of their lives binding them together. Perhaps her father still resented the time he had lost with his wife to this family, and now he had to share his daughter with them, too.

She left the three men sitting in tense silence as she went to prepare the final part of the meal. She had been so looking forward to this particular aspect, experimenting with batch after batch while Ivan was at work until she had the recipe down pat. She remembered her mother doing the same thing when she started working for Mrs. Friedman, who had been a kind but exacting woman. If you couldn't make latkes to her specifications, you had to go.

As Sofie pulled the schmaltz out of the fridge, having hidden it behind the okra where Ivan would never venture, she thought of the standoff in the living room and felt like all her preparation would come to naught. But then she remembered all the times she had almost let despair win the day. If giving up was the way to go, the Civil Rights Act wouldn't have passed just that summer, beginning what was hopefully a brighter day for the children she and Ivan might one day have.

Sofie reached into the cabinet and pulled down the little plastic recipe box. Her name was inscribed on the label in fading black ink. The handwriting was so similar to her own that it still threw her off at first sight, until she remembered it belonged to the woman who was little more than a patchwork quilt of memories and emotions: her mother.

She pulled out the recipe and stared at it for a moment. That this was in her possession was, in a small way, responsible for Ivan coming into her life. She gave the creased index card a kiss for luck before reading the instructions she had already committed to memory. Her movements were automatic now: she lit the tabletop range, placed the cast iron skillet on the flames, and added a healthy coating of schmaltz to the pan. She began spooning in the mix of grated potatoes, onion, and egg a dollop at a time, spreading it out into flat discs.

If this didn't appease them, at least she could say she hadn't gone down without a fight.

Things were no better when she bought out the platter of piping hot latkes. Ivan shot her a look of desperate relief when she came back into the room, and rushed to relieve her of the bowls of sour cream and applesauce she balanced precariously on each forearm.

"Happy Hanukkah," he said quietly as he took the bowls from her and dropped a kiss on her church. There was no sarcasm in his voice; he meant it.

They sat at the table, no one making eye contact. The dreidel lay unspun. The shamash flickered away at the center of the menorah, the lone candle on the rightmost side still unlit.

"Well, dig in!" she said in her bright hostess voice, even though she was tense enough that her jaw was starting to cramp. The men began stuffing their mouths, seemingly happy to have something to do to end the awkward silence.

Ivan made a sound of pleasurable surprise when he bit into his first latke. For a moment she thought she had made some miscalculation: too many onions or too little salt, or the schmaltz had gone bad. But when she glanced at him, he was regarding her with such adoration that it seemed too intimate for the dinner table. He didn't say anything, but his eyes were wide as he slowly chewed, savoring the taste.

"Sofie." Mr. Friedman cleared his throat. His eyes were glossy beneath his shaggy brows when he looked her full in the face for the first time that night. With his defenses down and his brow unlined, the similarity between him and his son was remarkable. "This tastes like…" He paused and pressed his lips together.

"Your mother's," her dad said quietly at the same time Mr. Friedman rasped out, "My wife's."

There was a silence around the table. Sofie dropped her hand into the space between her and Ivan's seats. His hand was waiting, as she knew it would be, and the sweet relief that coursed through her when his fingers slid between hers made her throat tight with emotion.

Mr. Friedman stood and walked toward the menorah. He lifted the shamash with trembling hands and began singing the first blessing in a soft but commanding voice as he lit the first candle of Hanukkah. "*Barukh atah Adonai, Eloheinu, melekh ha'olam…*"

When Ivan's deep voice joined his father's, when her own father reached across the table for both of their hands and joined the blessing on the only word he could make out of the Hebrew—*Amein*—she finally understood what that term "mitzvah" meant. It was the kindness that allowed people to overcome all the differences society had erected as walls between them. It was a shared memory of love that could bridge what seemed to be an insurmountable gap. It was being surrounded by those that she cared about most, and knowing that, against all hardship, they were going to make it.

No Valley Low

February 14, 1973

Cleveland, Ohio

Ivan fought the monotonous lullaby of the Ford Falcon's engine as the car rumbled through the invisible barrier that separated Shaker Heights from the other Cleveland neighborhoods. Fatigue was pushing at him from all sides, like a flurry of jabs while he was pinned up in the corner of the ring. Or maybe it was the bits of his past packed into boxes that clinked and rattled in the back seat that gave the car an oppressive air.

He cranked down the window down and let some of the icy winter air smack him in the face to revive him for this last stretch of his trip. He'd been driving for ten hours, through snow and over icy roads, leaving Richmond and the memories that had kept him company for the last three weeks in his rearview mirror.

His father was settled in his new wife, Mrs. Edelman, whose years of doting on the widower Friedman had finally led to a second chance at love for them both. Ivan was happy for his father, even if it still felt slightly uncomfortable, like he was being forced to wear necktie to work. Ivan's childhood home had been emptied of everything that connected him to it and put on the market.

So it goes, he thought.

The trip had been hard, but good. He'd had a chance to check in with Jack, his old boxing coach, who'd retired and now spent his time doting on his grandkids and bugging Ivan to open his own gym. He'd spent a few nights with his father-in-law, arguing politics and religion. He'd even helped his father around the shop like he had when he was a kid, and had the shock of his life when his dad asked him how Ivan kept things going strong with Sofie.

"What with the look?" his father has asked, incredulous. "I haven't been married since Eisenhower was in office."

Ivan wasn't sure he liked having his father ask him for advice instead of giving it unsolicited, but he'd rattled off some tripe about staying interested, about making sure to be there for your wife. Now he was heading home to Sofie, and he couldn't stop wondering if he'd been describing the husband he was or the husband he wished he could be.

There had been distance between him and Sofie in the weeks leading up to his departure. Months if he was honest. A quick smooch in the hallway as she ran to emergency meetings at the Women for Women clinic. A note left on the kitchen table before he headed out to another rally anti-war rally. There'd been sex; satisfying, but more perfunctory than passionate. They'd just been too damn busy. At least that's what he told himself.

But now the Peace Accords had been signed and the war was over. *Roe* v. *Wade* had meant a victory for women all over the US. Their battles were seemingly done, and they were left to face the unspoken thing they'd buried under newspapers, protest signs, and piles of paperwork over the last several months. Now they'd have to face each other without the padding of politics.

Maybe everything would be different now. In the past three weeks, the world had changed a hell of a lot. There was no reason that shouldn't be the same when he stepped over the threshold into their home.

Under the noise of the engine, Ivan heard the familiar strains of guitar and reached for the radio's volume knob just in time to catch Marvin's smooth voice keen,

Ain't no mountain high,
Ain't no valley low,
Ain't no river wide enough, baby.

Ivan felt a little tremor go through him when Tammi Terrel's sweet voice countered with, *If you need me, call me...*

It was funny how life with Sofie had changed him. Back before he'd met her, the only music that'd mattered to him was the chime of ringside bells, the syncopated pummel of glove against skin. Now, he listened closely to the singers when a song came on. He caught the intake of breath before an explosive burst of sound. He traced the emotions that could be expressed by how many times a long note trembled. And now he knew what Sofie sounded like singing along to all the pop songs of a decade plus; listening without her wasn't the same.

Sofie's mood ring made a tinkling sound in the little receptacle below the radio as it rolled against some pennies. She'd taken it off after that trip to the doctor all those months ago, saying she didn't need a damned ring to tell her how bad she felt.

Ivan turned the volume up a bit more.

You don't have to worry, Tammi sang, her voice radiating comfort.

No matter how many times he heard the song, it always took him back to one moment in time. It was back in their first apartment together, the one Sofie had made bright and cheerful despite the occasional swastika or racial slur scrawled on their door. He'd come home after a bad day of sparring at the gym. His reflexes had been slow, his opponent faster. For the first time, the fact that maybe he had a peak, and that he'd reached it, occurred to him. That boxing wasn't a career a man like him could support a family with, and that maybe the odd construction jobs he took on would soon be everyday life for him. Resentment had filled him, left him angry at anything and everything, but then he'd walked into their apartment at just the right moment. He'd heard Sofie's muffled voice, singing as usual, as he turned the key in the lock, and when he walked in she'd turned to him with all the love she felt for him shining in her eyes and finished the last line of the verse.

You don't have to worry.

The words hadn't magically changed his world, but they'd washed over him like the truth. That had been enough until he figured out his next step.

When was the last time she sang for me? Or I made her smile?

Ivan clenched his big hands tight around the steering wheel, glancing at the flowers and chocolate in the passenger seat. He and Sofie had made it through so much. Marches against injustice. The splintering of the movement. X, King, Kennedy. The years of worry that his draft number would be called and he'd be sent to die in a jungle, or to jail for refusing. His trips criss-crossing the country for the anti-war movement. Hers ferrying desperate women all over, sometimes to Chicago, sometimes to New York—anywhere they could receive help that was safer than a wire hanger. When was the last time they'd taken a moment to just enjoy the act of being together?

Being an activist wasn't easy, and being a married activist was a hell of a lot harder.

Ivan sometimes wondered how many hours they'd given to other people; he was sure Sofie kept a running tally, along with the other lists that had become a part of his everyday life: *Monthly Organization Meetings; Draft Dodger Resources; Women's Health Center Networks; Days since Last Period.*

He glanced at the flowers and candy again once. Maybe he should have gotten her jewelry, too? He was no good at this. He knew Sofie didn't care about Valentine's Day, but he wanted to make her happy, dammit.

The familiar oak tree that was growing up through the sidewalk in front of Mr. Lyons's house was illuminated by the light of his car. Almost home. Dirty snow clung to the curbs of the suburban street. One of the neighborhood kids had outlined a crude penis in the snow that dusted Mrs. Davidson's windshield. Or maybe it had been Sofie; the woman was the only one in the racially mixed cul de sac who insisted on making her prejudices known.

The rude neighbor was forgotten as their small aluminum-sided house appeared in front of him, and a familiar feeling threatened to overwhelm him. He wasn't good with words, but he didn't think there was one in

English to describe it, or Yiddish either. It wasn't love, or lust, or anything pedestrian like that. It was knowing that Sofie was close and soon he'd see that familiar smile, her deep brown eyes, and maybe the crease that formed between her brows when he said something just to push her buttons. That crease had prefaced a lot of good times for them. Ivan hadn't teased it into appearing for months now, though.

He sighed, struggled with the door, and then grabbed the flowers and candy on his way out. The bags and boxes of memories could wait in the car. He was more concerned with the future.

He opened the door and was greeted by a crown of dark ringlets bent over a pile of blocks in the hallway. At the sound of his footstep on the hardwood floor, the head popped up and he was met with a drooly, snaggletoothed grin.

"Hi." The greeting was said with the cute nonchalance of a human just learning to speak that slayed Ivan every time.

"Hey, buddy," Ivan said as he hung up his coat and started down the hall. The voices of two women could be heard from the kitchen.

"He's been so withdrawn." Not Sofie speaking, thank goodness. "Sometimes it's like he's still out in the jungle for all the response I can get from him. But I'm just glad he's alive."

Ivan paused next to the toddler, his leg serving as a support as baby Paul wrapped his arm around Ivan's calf and pulled himself to his feet.

"I-ben." Paul held up his small hand and Ivan took it. He tried not to squeeze the soft little mitt hard. Tried not to remember Sofie curled up into a ball in the center of their bed, sobbing for a loss he could never feel as keenly as her. He was sure a part of them had been left in their bedroom that day, when he'd struggled for the right words and had found only silence. Now that things were calm…he hoped that they'd be able to retrieve whatever it was, or to form something new, stronger, to replace it.

The reticence and fatigue he'd been feeling dropped away when he stepped into the kitchen, replaced by the deep-rooted nostalgia and heady hit of new appreciation he always experienced when he hadn't seen her for a while.

She was leaning back against the counter, arms crossed over her chest and head tilted in that way she had of making people feel like she was really listening to them. Her brown corduroy pants belled out at the hem, but the flare at her hips was more than a trend: it was all Sofie. A tan blouse, tucked in and belted, completed the look. Her hair was pulled up into the afropuff ponytail style he thought made her look even younger than her years.

She was nodding at their neighbor, Marjorie, when her gaze swung to him. A bright smile lit up her face and suddenly they were dumb kids again, or even dumber teenagers. Her smile faltered when she glanced at his hand clutching Paul's, but she shook it off like a boxer acting as if a jab hadn't left him dazed for a second.

Marjorie's gaze swung between Sofie and Ivan and a conspiratorial grin lit her face. She brushed a shock of blond fringe out of her eyes. "Welcome home, Mr. Friedman. I'll be on my way now. It's almost bedtime for this little guy and his daddy is supposed to tuck him in." She was through the kitchen in a few steps, then swooped up her little boy, blowing a raspberry on his brown belly that sent him into a fit of giggles. "Later, Sof. I'll leave you two to…catch up." She winked at Ivan and then trotted down the hallway.

"Bye, Marj," Sofie called out after her, but a gust of cold wind and the slamming of the door signaled they were alone.

She stared at Ivan and he wished he could read her as well as he could the opponents he used to fight. Then, he'd been able to tell when a blow was coming, even if he couldn't dodge it. But he couldn't understand the flash of apprehension in her eyes now that they were alone. She'd had time to think over the last few weeks, too. What if her thoughts had led her to a different conclusion?

She finally walked over and gave him a kiss on the cheek; behind all her dynamite moves she was still shy with him sometimes. Sometimes it felt like a good thing, but Ivan wasn't sure this was one of those times. When she took his hand and led him to the love seat in the living room, he let himself relax a bit.

"How's the old man?" she asked. "Or old men, rather. Did you give your dad my housewarming gift?"

Ivan laughed, remembering his father's expression when he'd unwrapped the small framed print that said "I'm black and I'm proud." His dad had laughed, and Ivan had been glad that his wife and his father were friendly enough to joke about things now. It hadn't always been that way.

"Oh yeah. It's hung in a place of honor. Right next to the picture of Nixon."

Sofie grinned. "I know your father has his issues, but even he wouldn't torture himself like that."

"Not him. My stepmother apparently thinks Nixon has a certain sex appeal."

Sofie's eyes widened. "No."

"I wish I was joking," Ivan said. He frowned. "I certainly didn't need to hear the words 'sex appeal' from the mouth of a woman who used to pinch my cheeks before temple."

Sofie let out a peal of laughter, and the sound allowed Ivan to relax a bit more. "'Nixon' and 'sex appeal' shouldn't be in the same solar system let alone the same sentence, but I'll try to reserve judgment."

There was a silence as they looked at each other, letting the novel lightness of their mood just be. They examined each other, taking in the changes of the last few weeks. The last few months. There was lots to talk about, but Ivan had spent the last few weeks drowning in memories. Every part of Richmond had reminded him of Sofie, and now he was readjusting to her as she was in the moment: beautiful, strong, and still crazy enough to stick with a schmuck like him.

"Are those for me?" She motioned to the gifts he was clutching in his other hand and it was only then he remembered it was Valentine's Day, not Stare at Your Wife Day.

"Oh yeah." He handed them over. "Nothing but the best for my lady. These were purchased at the finest Texaco in all of Ohio."

"What a lady killer," she said in a faux breathy voice as she accepted. She sniffed the flowers. "Diesel? You shouldn't have."

"Premium, baby," he said, sliding his arm over her shoulders. He let the familiar shape of her against him, of them on their couch, take hold of him. Things felt…normal. "I want to take you out for dinner, but this will have to do for now."

Sofie pressed herself closer to him by a fraction of an inch. "I'd rather stay in, if you don't mind. I feel like we haven't done this in forever. Just sat and…existed. Together." His arm rose and fell as she sighed deeply. "I'll have a chocolate, though." She pulled off the top of the shiny red cardboard heart, and Ivan watched as her features pulled into the same helpless expression she always wore when she fought against emotion. Her gaze flew to his.

"Where did this come from?" She settled the box on her lap and grabbed up the picture on top of the stack of photos that had replaced the chocolates at the center. She stared at the photo in awe, and all the heaving and sweating and aching of the house clearing Ivan had done was worth it in that moment.

"I found them in a box of my mom's stuff in the basement," he said. "I don't remember this day at all, do you?"

"No," she said, smiling as she shuffled through. "We were always making up games like this."

His mother had probably snapped the photos of young Sofie and Ivan playing in the Friedman's backyard after she received a Kodak Tourist camera from his dad for her fortieth birthday. She'd fancied herself a photographer for a few weeks in the summer of '54, taking photos of everything—apparently, sometimes without the knowledge of her subjects.

Ivan watched as Sofie examined each photo. In one, they both had their arms spread like birds taking flight. In another, they appeared to be in conversation with an invisible person who was much shorter than them.

Ivan rested his free hand on Sofie's thigh as they flipped through the memories because even though she was tucked against him, he still needed more of her. "We were pretty cute, huh?"

"You still are," she said, glancing at him with a sweet smile. "Sometimes."

He squeezed her thigh and she giggled.

"These were taken before you chipped your tooth, so we're what? Ten?" She shuffled to the next photo, and her hand shook a bit. In the picture, a young Sofie held a long stick pointed toward a young Ivan. Her eyes were squinted against the sun as she issued some command. Ivan had his hands in the air and was smiling at her like she was the best thing since sliced bread. Stepping into the frame was Sofie's mother, his family's help back then, a look of amused exasperation on her face as she reached for the stick from behind Sofie.

In the next photo, Ivan was chasing Sofie out of the frame. Her mother was staring straight into the camera, stick in hand, sharing a knowing smile with her photographer.

"I really look like her," Sofie said. "Don't I? Here, in the cheeks and eyes?"

"You do," he agreed.

"Sometimes I forget what she looked like." She took a deep breath, then placed the photos neatly on the table beside the couch before turning and kissing him on the lips. She was soft and warm and smelled of the Raveen hair product she used that he wasn't allowed to touch. He'd once bought a jar of the pomade while on the road, just to get a whiff of her. He hadn't told her that, though—he'd said it was on sale so he picked it up for her. A man had to have some secrets from his wife.

She pulled away and looked at him like he was the alpha and the omega. "Thank you, Ivan. This is…well, I know I told you Sidney Poitier was the perfect man, but maybe, just maybe, I was mistaken."

"I think he's perfect, too, but I'm a pretty swell consolation prize," Ivan said as she stood and walked to the other side of the room. He leaned back against the soft pillow of the couch, watching her. "It's funny, the games we used to play when we were kids. We were always fighting against injustice—invading aliens or evil kings—even back then. I guess we really are a perfect match, huh?"

Sofie was walking back to him now, a flat gift-wrapped box in her hands.

"Guess?" The crease formed between her brows.

"Let me rephrase," he said holding up a hand as she sat down. "We really are a perfect match."

"Damn right, we are," she said, raising her brows at him. She sat the box on his lap and looked at him expectantly.

He unwrapped the perfectly tied ribbon, then ripped through the carefully taped and folded wrapping paper. Her fidgeting leg shook the couch a little as he removed the lid and stared down at the silky gold boxing shorts decorated with white trim.

"Thanks, baby, but these are a bit small, don't you think?" he asked with an incredulous laugh as he lifted the tiny, meticulously sewn shorts out. "These are small enough for a—"

Everything came together as he read the words stitched below the waistline: BABY FRIEDMAN.

His head turned to her, whiplash fast. "Sof."

His heart thudded so hard in his ears that he almost didn't hear her shaky inhale. This wasn't the first time they'd sat like this, her sharing the happy news with him. The part of his brain that remembered what happened later, that dark day in their bedroom, the part that remembered their crushed dreams, fought against the joy that surged through him, but his fear was nothing against the love and happiness that crashed through him.

"Sof." He said her name again because he still couldn't find the words.

"I didn't want to tell you until…until the odds were better." She was crying, but not tears of sadness. He was crying, too, he realized, and he couldn't wipe away the tears because both of their hands were joined between them. When had that happened?

"I thought maybe I'd missed a couple of months because of the stress and the travel and the work. I chalked the nausea up to stress, too." She shook her head. "Maybe I didn't want to know, so I could handle it better if nothing came of it. But I went to my doctor last week and we're three months along."

"Sofie." He pulled her against him and hugged her, tight. He didn't know what to say, still, but he'd learned that sometimes it was what you didn't say that messed everything up. Being silent wasn't an option this time. "I love you. And, look, I know I messed up last time. I'm sorry I didn't know what to say when you were in pain, back then. I was paralyzed, and I wasn't there for you. And then I felt like I couldn't get you back because of it. But

I'm here no matter what happens this time. I won't let you down."

She pulled back, confusion etched in her expression. "What do you mean? You *were* there for me. You held my hand. You brought me tea and brushed my hair, and made sure I was comfortable. I wouldn't have gotten through it without you. After…after it was over, you left me little notes every day. You tried. *I* was the one who didn't want to talk, who couldn't look you in the eye. I felt like a failure. Or like I'd been punished, or our baby had been punished for me."

She sucked in a breath. "I didn't even really know I was thinking that until I said it."

Ivan's heart twisted that she'd been in such pain and he hadn't known. It had never even occurred to him that she might be feeling guilt instead of disappointment in him. "I've never thought you were a failure," he said, cupping her face and brushing a thumb over her cheek. "Not ever. Come on, you're amazing! It's so obvious to me that maybe I haven't made it as clear as I should have."

They stared at each other for a moment as the events of the last several months realigned themselves in the light of this new understanding. The awkward silences. The stiff kisses. The stuttering conversations. And then they burst out laughing. It was morbid, inappropriate, and exactly what they needed in that moment.

"Seriously? You mean, all of this time?" Ivan heaved between breaths.

"We were both blaming ourselves?" Sofie finished for him with a high-pitched squeak.

They let out a howl of laughter, one that purged the guilt and the fear as everything that had been wrong between them slowly shifted back towards being right.

"This is gonna be one lucky kid, you know," Ivan said when they'd finally calmed down and lay slouched against each other on the couch. He eased a hand down to rest on her still flat belly and she laced her fingers through his.

"Why? Because his parents will fight anyone and everyone to make the world a better place for him?" she asked.

"Well, that," Ivan said with a shrug, "but I was thinking she'll get to celebrate Hanukkah *and* Christmas. And have the best shorts in her gym class."

Sofie gave him her creased brow look and swatted at him. "You're incorrigible." Her full lips pulled up into a smile that said she didn't see that particular trait as a problem. "And you've also been gone three weeks."

She stood and began walking toward the stairs that led to their bedroom, her fingers busy with the buttons of her shirt. Ivan didn't move, watching the coordinated sway of her hips as she walked up the steps.

Sway. Button pop. Sway. Button pop.

When she was out of sight on the upstairs landing, her shirt came fluttering down over the banister to land in a heap on the living room floor.

I am one lucky chump, he thought as he stood and hustled toward the stairs.

"Are you going to keep me waiting, Mr. Friedman?

"You don't have to worry about that, Mrs. Friedman."

He took the stairs two by two.

author's note

Thank you so much for reading! I hope you enjoyed Sofie and Ivan's story—these two crazy kids have been bouncing around in my head for years and I'm happy that I was finally able to bring them out into the light. If you'd like to learn more about the Freedom Rides, I suggest the following resources:

- Etheridge, Eric, Roger Wilkins, and Diane McWhorter. 2008. *Breach of peace: portraits of the 1961 Mississippi freedom riders*. New York: Atlas & Co.
- Arsenault, Raymond. 2006. *Freedom riders: 1961 and the struggle for racial justice*. Oxford: Oxford University Press.
- American Experience: Freedom Riders. 2011. PBS. This documentary is available online at http://www.pbs.org/wgbh/americanexperience/freedomriders/.

If you enjoyed this story and would like to read more of my multicultural historicals, check out *Agnes Moor's Wild Knight*, the story of a black woman and her Highlander in medieval Scotland, and *Be Not Afraid*, an African-American Revolutionary War romance.

If you'd like to get updates about new releases and access to exclusive reads, sign up for my newsletter at http://bit.ly/ac-news.

Best,
Alyssa

about the author

Alyssa Cole is a science editor, pop culture nerd, and romance junkie who lives in the Caribbean and occasionally returns to her fast-paced NYC life. When she's not busy traveling and learning French, she can be found watching cat videos on the Internet with her real-life romance hero. Contact her on Twitter at @alyssacolelit or visit her online at www.AlyssaCole.com.

CPSIA information can be obtained at www.ICGtesting.com
Printed in the USA
LVOW07s2320140916

504678LV00005B/154/P